The Pumpkin Season

Dan Anthony

The Pumpkin Season
Dan Anthony

ISBN 978-1903110805

First published in this edition 2021 by Wrecking Ball Press

Design: humandesign.co.uk

Supported using public funding by
**ARTS COUNCIL
ENGLAND**
LOTTERY FUNDED

TUESDAY, OCTOBER 1ST

It was October, the pumpkin season. Gregor, the fictitious detective, reviewed his observations for the day. A plot is what an investigation requires and, as far as he could make out, there was no plot. There was nothing worth considering other than, perhaps, his own motives for seeking a plot amongst the unsurprising actions of all who lived around him.

That morning there had been a robbery and he had almost witnessed it. About two hundred metres from his flat there was a rather down-at-heel shop, selling newspapers, cigarettes, dusty bottles of water, dry-looking apples and sun-bleached tins of peaches, pineapples and prunes. Every day, before work, Gregor called to pick up his newspaper. When he arrived on this particular morning there was pandemonium in the place, as if an invisible devil had been let loose amongst the articles for sale.

Karen, the owner, was sobbing. Five minutes earlier, a stranger had walked in, produced a knife and demanded the contents of the till. But as Gregor listened to her tale, his fingers twitched restlessly on the counter top. He was impatient to get on with it – the day, which like all others, would have nothing in it. He waited as Karen told him how a thin, ferret-faced young man, with hair like wire wool and eyes like a dying eel, sprang into her world clutching a blade and demanding money. Why, she asked, would anybody want to rob her shop? The place turned over next to nothing. Gregor nodded. She was the latest in a long line of hapless shopkeepers who, perhaps because of their inability to sell things, had opted for the little place positioned just off the main road on an almost disused cut through.

The robber could not have taken enough money to buy a train ticket, thought Gregor. He glanced around him: that tired little place with its aging commodities and its outmoded till wasn't worthy of a plot. It was an exhibit in the gallery of failure. He muttered that the robber was most likely to have been a junkie and that his knife had probably been stolen from a restaurant. Karen seized on Gregor's words. The chosen weapon was, indeed, a carving knife. She remembered the panic in the man's eyes, his tremulous grip on the handle of his blade, the horrible feeling that her life was in the hands of a madman whose judgement was impaired, who couldn't be relied upon to react to anything in a predictable way.

Gregor handed Karen a twenty, which she could not change. He said she should keep it but she accepted the gift with reluctance. She said she didn't like to and that she'd give him his change when he next came in. But Gregor insisted that he didn't want any change, somehow the overpayment seemed the least he could do to restock the till. Then the police arrived.

The cops called more cops. Two of them produced semi-automatic weapons and bounded off in the direction the thief had taken. Karen and Gregor watched from the doorway, unimpressed. The policemen ran like a pair of cheetahs chasing an antelope in a wildlife documentary, in slow motion. They bounded like spacemen in space suits on the surface of the moon. As soon as they reached the junction with the main road they stopped, they could not tell which way to turn. They slowed to a histrionic halt.

Another car arrived. A plain clothes inspector stepped out. He wore a grey Italian suit and a tie with a silver clip in the shape of a race car. It was an old Bugatti, or perhaps an Alfa Romeo. It looked like a long, streamlined cigar with a driver cowering down behind the engine, almost obscured by the spinning rear wheel and a stylised trail of exhaust fumes. The inspector surveyed the shop with the same eyes that the estate agent used in the same place every time someone went bust. A junkie in a shithole, a bloody waste of time. He took a statement from Karen and ordered his men to set up bollards and put up tape outside the shop front. Then he left.

Gregor passed on his commiserations and continued his journey to work, secretly thinking that a true plot requires more depth, there was nothing for him to investigate at the shop. As he walked, he wondered what the robbery signified and whether there were any lessons that could be learned. Perhaps he should consider the business of walking home alone at night more attentively; after all, if they didn't catch the junkie he might return. Perhaps, and this seemed a worryingly likely possibility to Gregor, given the obvious stupidity of the young man, he might go back return to the shop to see if he could find more money – maybe Gregor's twenty. Gregor made a mental note to be more vigilant, he shouldn't have left the note.

Later, in his office, Gregor reviewed the remainder of the day's events. Nothing had occurred that couldn't have happened on any other day. His newspaper, spread out on his desk, confirmed this. So, as usual, Gregor left for home with a bundle of files and no plot worthy of the name.

*   *   *

Clara sang as she drove. Her bus was empty. Sometimes she forgot to check and she found herself singing at the top of her voice to an audience of bemused passengers. But now she knew she was alone. The number 37 route at 6.30 pm on the return leg back from the Black Forest into town always was. It was an empty part of town.

'And then I went and spoiled it all by saying something stupid like I love you.'

She jabbed on the breaks. They hissed and the bus (which was quite new) lunged to an immediate halt. A black BMW had leaped out from a side street.

'Bastard!' yelled Clara, flashing her lights.

'I'm a fucking bus. I could crush you like a head louse.'

The first time Clara discovered a head-louse in her son's hair it was a shock. There, amongst the fine wisps of clean light brown hair was this black creature. It may as well have been a BMW. She pulled it out, understanding instantly that this was a serious moment in her life. It was the first time she had identified anything that was against her son. The head-louse, pincered between her fingers, wanted to harm the boy. Others, like her ex might, through thoughtlessness, laziness or stupidity pose an unwitting danger. They weren't malicious. Her ex always professed love for his son; he always said he wanted to do the right thing. This head-louse, on the other hand, was intentionally provocative: it wanted war, it could not compromise, its job was to louse things up.

She hoped that the head-louse was a loner, a lost traveller or an outcast, but she knew, deep down, that such lice are very rare. It was more likely that the head-louse was part of a gang, some of whom were watching her. She had an infestation on her hands. The next morning she phoned in sick, and then rang the crèche and told them her son had a temperature. And so, shame faced, because none of us like nits, she went to the pharmacy and stocked up on an arsenal of chemical weapons which she secretly rubbed into her screaming son's scalp at bath time, reassuring herself by reading and re-reading the small print on all the labels, all which said the stuff was safe to use, if precautions were taken. Before returning her son to the crèche, Clara felt guilty. In spite of the notices on the walls instructing parents to inform the staff if they found head-lice in their children's hair, Clara kept quiet. After all – isn't that what the parents of the bastard who brought the damn things in in the first place did? Clara felt guilty though. She felt as if she was passing herself and her boy off as normal, when she knew that they'd both been messing around with head-lice. The other mums and dads and their children all seemed so well organised and successful. The head-louse thing was not something she wanted to talk about, especially since she had dealt with it.

But a week or so later, something happened that changed everything: she found another head-louse. This time the discovery of the parasite was different. Not only was the sight of the creature not quite so shocking, Clara also felt a twinge of nostalgia for something familiar, a degree of self-confidence born out of experience and a grudging ripple of respect for a formidable enemy that did not know when it was beaten. With the air of an expert she squished the head-louse between her thumb and index finger, bought the chemicals, reluctantly applied them and sent her boy back to the crèche.

When she came to pick the boy up, one of the mothers tugged at her arm as they waited in the brightly coloured corridor.

'Have you had any... trouble?' asked the mother, raising her eye brows and holding a strand of her long red hair between the scarlet painted thumb and index finger nails of her right hand.

With some relief Clara confessed. She knew what the woman was talking about, the beasts kept coming back. Another parent, a man in a blue suit, who always seemed to be checking his watch, overheard them. He moaned about the head-lice and the fact that someone in the crèche kept infecting the others. Before long, all the waiting parents were debating head-lice. It seemed that they each of them had been suffering in silence. Eventually, everybody agreed that, that night, they would wash all their children's hair with lice killing chemicals, even though the health warnings printed on the side of the bottles worried them profoundly. They even formed a kind of committee, some of whom went back into the building to ask the crèche manager to forgive them for not coming forwards earlier and to promote the attack on the head-lice with new notices about the current infestation, but she declined, fearing that alarmist news of the infestation would deter new customers.

For a few weeks all the children were fine. But slowly rumours began to spread. Certain parents, it was alleged, were not continuing to wash their children's hair in the special medicated shampoo, which smelt like liquorice, for the duration of the treatment, because they thought it was dangerous. The writing on the side of the purple bottles, stating that the shampoo should be applied only when the shampooer was wearing gloves, worried many of them. The translucent skin of their young offspring looked so permeable. Their big hands felt as if they were covered in rhino hide by comparison. In the purple gloves that came with the bottles they looked like mad professor's hands. Surely it was wrong to wear gloves? Most of the parents could see that if they didn't all treat their children in the same way, it was only a matter of time before the lice returned so they held their noses, and their children, and persevered. When the lice came back, there was uproar. Someone was cheating.

It was Clara who had made the suggestion. Using chemical weapons on the head-lice was the wrong way to go forwards. They needed to take a leaf out of the Partisan's book, or any other practitioner of guerrilla war. They couldn't win by bombing the jungle– they had to get inside it. They abandoned their weapon of mass destruction, preferring traditional, organic brush and squash methods, fighting from follicle to follicle. Clara smiled as she remembered those hunts through her son's fine forest of fresh hair. She recalled her sense of triumph when she discovered the eggs. They never completely destroyed all of the lice but they made life so difficult for them that, in the end, the head-lice marched away.

Now, as the BMW inched its nose into the oncoming traffic in the opposite lane Clara wanted to squash it between her bus and a wall, like a louse between her nails. She flashed her lights again and swore at the two shadowy forms in the front seats of the black car. An arm was raised casually, as a gap appeared in the oncoming traffic and, with a squawk of rubber, the car drove off. How Clara wanted to feel the yielding sensation of that black metallic exoskeleton. She drove on a little and tapped the brakes again. She'd almost missed a stop and, miraculously, there was somebody standing there.

* * *

'Of course I want to fuck you,' said Niko. 'I just can't do it tonight.'
He sighed and looked impatiently out of the window as he wedged
the phone between his ear and his shoulder.

'Of course I love you, I just can't... it's not that I don't want to. I
just can't.... What do you mean 'I'm getting annoyed?' Of course I'm
not annoyed, it's just that I'm looking after the old man, I've got to
finish that project for geography... No,' he said.

The streetlights below shone up through the yellowing foliage
in the trees on the square outside. Huge leaf-like shadows rippled
across the walls of the apartment block opposite. Niko found
himself watching them, wondering why he had never noticed them
before. They looked like monsters. His girlfriend stopped speaking;
he wasn't entirely sure what she had just said. He guessed.

'I would definitely prefer to fuck you more than I would like to
write an essay about integrated transport systems. I would prefer
to make love to you more than anything. It's just that I can't fuck
and write at the same time. So I think you may as well get on with
something useful instead. And anyway, I've got to look after...'

Niko's voice tailed off, Laura was talking again. This time he
turned away from the window.

'Yes I love you,' he stated. He found himself speaking slowly and
loudly, 'I really, really do love just you. You are all I can think about,
for every waking hour of the day and all I dream about in the night,
and I particularly dream about fucking you, although, obviously we
do other stuff too, like go walking by the river and go to restaurants
and have holidays in... Corsica.'

Laura queried this. Niko, who was getting into his stride,
frowned, his brown eyes flashing with frustration.

'Why Corsica? I don't know. It's a nice place. They've got good beaches. It's always hot. It would be like our island. Our Romantic Island. Where we could talk and maybe go to museums and learn about the history and make Corsican love to Corsican music.'

Niko sighed, he sat down on a high stool next to three saucepans on the cooker. He pushed his hand into his long floppy brown hair.

'No, you can't come here. I certainly can't fuck you here, now... Because the old man is here and I'm looking after him. He's lying in bed. I have to feed him mashed up pumpkin soup, and sometimes a mashed banana, although he doesn't like those – they're good for him.'

Niko waved his arm over the carnage of chopped pumpkins and bananas strewn across the kitchen worktop. He continued, warming to his task, describing the scenario as if he was a journalist marching through a disaster area.

'He calls for me every ten minutes. It wouldn't be right. We've got pumpkins all over the place, we've got restaurant-scale quantities of soup. The whole place is sticky and covered in pips. And besides, although he can hardly speak, his ears are like a bat's. It wouldn't be right.'

Niko pulled his breadknife from the flesh of a halved, basketball-sized pumpkin and gently agitated some simmering soup. It was almost done. Big bubbles burst through the orange crust of the soup, leaving dimples and craters which Niko smoothed away.

'For fuck's sake, listen,' he shouted. 'We've got tomorrow, the day after tomorrow, the day after the day after tomorrow. We can go out, stay in, go to the pictures, we can buy a bottle of wine, get drunk and fuck all night. I'm cooking soup, looking after my grandfather and writing about transport systems tonight. Is that so very, very bad?'

His expression changed. Laura had said something that struck a nerve.

'Pumpkin soup sex?' he asked, 'what's that?'

*   *   *

Clara watched the woman take a seat. She lit a cigarette.

'Hey,' shouted Clara. 'This is a no-smoking bus.'

The woman glared at Clara, she took a long drag and then, somewhat histrionically, put the cigarette out on the floor with her thigh-high black leather boot.

'Sorry, I guess there's nobody else on the bus,' muttered Clara. 'We probably could have managed with a window.'

As she drove, Clara watched the woman through her mirror. It was unusual for tarts to use a bus and Clara wondered why this one had chosen hers. Her hair, dark, piled high like candy floss, was a meadow, with flowers and pastel-coloured hair clips scattered throughout. But her coat and boots were less romantic. They were expensive. Clara thought that they were probably Italian. The woman didn't appear to be down on her luck. Her coat, with its long folds of smooth leather, was a work of haute couture – the sort of thing a popstar would commission from a designer. Clara jerked the steering wheel as she drifted out of her lane. Her eyes were soon drawn back to the mirror. She liked that coat and the boots that went with it. Fuck-me boots and a fuck-you coat – a neat ensemble, thought Clara.

The further they drove; the more fascinated Clara became with her passenger and the less attention she paid to the road. This is no road-safety story though; Clara didn't crash. She caught a glimpse of the passenger's dark eyes, her white face and her old fashioned-looking rouged cheeks. This was not the lightless face of some loser trying to scrabble together the rent though fucking. This face was from the crowd at the Folies Bergère. The passenger was a work of art. Clara found herself beginning to appreciate the pinks, whites, blacks, yellows, violets, burgundies and aqua marines that buzzed around the fare's hair. It was as if her head was in a cloud of brightly coloured insects.

They stopped outside the Tivoli hotel. Clara leant on her steering wheel as the woman, half dusk and half dawn, stepped down from the bus, across the pavement and through the hotel door.

Clara depressed the accelerator and her bus slid away, leaving the grey walls and windows of the Tivoli Hotel behind. Later, as more passengers climbed on, Clara found herself preoccupied with the woman and her coat. What was she doing right now? Who could she be with?

The Tivoli Hotel was built in the 1950s, a solid and sombre precursor to the Etaps and Mercures that had mushroomed along the ring road more recently. It was once the most up-to-date hotel in town. Now, the latest news Clara had heard from the old Tivoli, from her grandmother, who still regarded grey concrete buildings with functional door fittings with the utmost respect, was that most of the top seven floors had been rented out to enterprises for office space. Clara's grandmother said that business was bad in the old place. Its redundant black marble ash trays, its heavy bronze mermaids and its metalwork, fading behind cataracts of dust, were decaying. The hotel was dying alone, like its guests. Now visitors' rooms and offices occupied the same corridors giving the place a constant air of semi-permanence. It was neither a true place of work, nor was it a good spot to go for a sleep. Everybody in the building tip-toed around one another because nobody knew who was really supposed to be there.

Most of the people who encountered the Tivoli's split personality were looking for somewhere else. They were reps from out of town attending conferences, unable to book into the modern places or perhaps teachers attending meetings who, for one reason or other, preferred to stay somewhere 'different' and maybe the occasional misguided tourist, anxious to soak up the atmosphere from a time most residents of the city preferred to forget. They all had to put up with the Tivoli's eccentricities: the presence of a small road haulage business in the next bedroom, for example, with its jangling telephones, its printers and its shredders, was unsettling, and at the same time, soothing for the insomniac a little further along the corridor, who, lying on a single bed, staring at the grey ceiling, never felt alone. Not only did it fail to provide a restful environment, the Tivoli also heightened a sensation that all travellers feel wherever they go: a sense of contextlessness. It exposed this in everyone – whether they were supposed to be there or not. Even if you were in context in the Tivoli, you felt out of place – as if life itself was naturally incongruous and order, or feeling in context, was a ridiculous idea. Everyone who stayed in the Tivoli felt this intense haplessness – more so than anywhere else. It was the Tivoli's unspoken unique selling point. Some people even came there because of it. Most guests assumed that this unease was enhanced by the fact that the hotel itself was in the process of collapse, of stopping being a hotel altogether, through a piecemeal disintegration which meant that it was arguably, already, not a true hotel. But the truth is, in the past, even when all its rooms were guest rooms, and its concrete walls were clean and new, in its heyday, all the visitors had the same feelings – as if both the place and its punters were pretending to be something which none of them could quite believe.

Surely, thought Clara as she drove away from the hotel, that Romantic vision from her bus would not be fucking some lost shopkeeper for the price of a bottle of hock in the Tivoli.

As Clara ploughed on through the moonlit night, three black shapes lodged in her imagination: the coat, the BMW and, by association, a head louse.

*   *   *

Laura bit deep into the cotton curtain and stifled, as best she could, a loud moan.

'Quiet', murmured Niko.

This was the one time when even he found speaking difficult. Laura moaned again, this time without the curtain, which had somehow passed her by. She stretched her arms forwards, grabbing the mantelpiece, pumpkin juice causing her hands to slip and slide on the neat wooden fitting like flippers on a rock.

'Oh fuck.... Oh fuck... FUCK,' she cried allowing her arms to float free, knocking over a standard lamp. Niko was just amazing.

Niko, who had discovered himself somehow separated from most of Laura by the curtain, pushed his head forwards up her slippery neck, under the pumpkin-spattered curtains, to find Laura's face. She twisted her head and they kissed as if they were eating each other.

'I love you,' whispered Laura.

'I don't think he heard,' grunted Niko.

Only when they stood up did Niko consider the possibility that he was probably wrong. The collateral damage was severe. Soup had spread from the kitchen into the small living room, the television lay on its side, the lamp on top of it had broken in two, the curtains hung at jaunty angles. A look of frustration crossed Niko's face: the place was upended and there was no essay on integrated transport systems.

Laura, on the other hand, naked, surveyed the devastation with pride. It was a sensuous soupy aftermath, in which household objects lay like broken canons on a battlefield. She loved the chaotic mash. Which was odd, because she was usually a very neat girl.

'Let me tell you what happened,' said Jani, pausing to take a sip of beer from his glass.

Three ragged faces ranged along the bar eyed Jani sceptically. This gentleman, who had just told the three men that he was called Jani, had contributed practically nothing to the evening other than to moan about the fact that he'd lost his phone. He listened and drank. Now, uplifted by an inexplicable and somewhat euphoric lack of inhibition, Jani filled his lungs with air, he pushed his chest forwards and spoke. The strangers in this strange bar could, perhaps, help him.

'Guess,' said Jani, with some pride, 'what I do.'

'You work in the university,' said one of the men.

Jani was a little disappointed.

'Well, close, very close, I'm a teacher. I teach geography. In fact, at half past eight tomorrow morning I will be standing in front of a group of students talking about integrated transport policies. What will be different about tomorrow will be this,' Jani held his hand up, commanding attention: 'tomorrow I will have a hangover. How did you guess I was in education?'

'You're wearing a check shirt and your jeans are too clean.'

'You have elbow patches on your sports jacket.'

'You have lost your mobile phone. Only someone in education would lose his mobile phone the way you did. You don't care that you've lost your phone. That means it's not important to you. When did anybody need to phone a teacher?'

'Well,' said Jani, slightly confused by the specificity of his audience's replies, 'I'm sure you can't guess my story.'

'Wanna bet?' said a man with a full beard and a thirst for gin. 'Your mistress has just thrown you out.'

Jani choked on his lager. Not because he was right, but because he called her his 'mistress'. It sounded old-fashioned. He looked around the bar noting its high ceiling and the ornate plaster mouldings thereon. The bar itself was also old-fashioned, also high with shiny mirrors and a plethora of glass, and the emblems of beer and spirit manufacturers.

'Ah!,' said the fattest of the three men, 'your wife is refusing to speak to you.'

Jani nodded glumly, all prospects of decanting his story with pride were lost.

'Now, that's where you are wrong: she still speaks to me, it's the language she uses that could do with an upgrade.'

'But she doesn't want you back.'

'No, not today,' said Jani.

'And you want to go back?'

'I live there, it's my home. My kids are there. I am their father. She should take me back because the alternative is worse.'

'For whom?' said the thinnest and oldest of the three men, the one with the long ashen face and the sad grey eyes.

'For everyone. OK. So I made a mistake, everyone makes mistakes. I mean, I'm no worse a person really. I was Jani before I had an affair and I'm still the same old Jani. But now I don't want to have an affair any more. In fact, you could say I'm a better version of myself because I've learned my lesson.'

'New improved Jani,' echoed the bearded man, whose nickname was Priest. 'He has the wisdom of Solomon.'

'Hey, what is this? Look at me. Do I look like a two-timing bastard?'

The men looked at one another. Teachers usually were, weren't they? It got them through the day.

'Yes,' they all said.

'Great,' said the teacher. 'I may as well have the words 'mother-fucker' tattooed on my forehead.'

'You don't do that too?' asked Priest, rolling a cigar beneath his ample nose.

'Of course not,' said Jani.

'Shame, it would be a better story if he did.'

'He shagged a student, that's all. Some beautiful seventeen-year-old got fed up with spotty seventeen-year-old wannabes and set her sights on something with a bit of class – someone with patches on his elbows,' countered the fat one. 'That may seem unbelievable to us at this time of night. But I bet, with a good night's kip and a bit of ironing he brushes up smart. Now, what would you do in his position? Pretend to be a monk or act honestly, on impulse. Opportunities like that do not come along very often. In fact, for some people, they never come at all. Do they, Smoke?'

The thin-faced man moved to the doorway and shook his head gravely.

'Put it like that and you've got no choice. You're damned if you do and damned if you don't. It's a very life-like paradox,' whispered the smoker, lighting his cigarette. 'In the end you've got no choice – you're damned – so you may as well grab what pleasures you can, because everything will be confiscated. Life is a matter of confiscation of privileges.'

Smoke pushed the door half open and puffed outside whilst retaining one foot inside and one ear on the conversation.

'So how did it end?' asked the fat one.

Jani opened his mouth, but again, Priest, who was still sniffing his cigar and scratching his beard, answered.

'He confessed,' exclaimed Priest. 'Like a fool he confessed, like a dumb peasant in front of some cardinal he confessed. He believed in all that baloney about owning up to sin, about being honest and true, about making a fresh start. But he forgot to whom he was confessing. He was confessing to his wife. Not a bloody priest. His wife! A real person!! Someone who had already decided that confession was for losers when she married him; someone who knows that in order to keep things on an even keel it isn't a good thing to confess anything to anyone un-priestly; someone who for the whole of her life has understood the fact that the truth is not something that bonds us, it is a weapon that kills us. Mrs Jani is far less forgiving than God or the priest. She's a real human being, not a professional one. She will not have seen Jani's confession as a testimony to his affection and respect for her; she will have seen it as an abdication of responsibility and a sign of weakness, giving up a secret like that is like passing a bomb to your neighbour – what's she supposed to do with it? There's nothing good in shipping on decisions and shirking responsibility. There are so many holes in your position that, as far as I can see, it resembles a piece of Swiss cheese. She will not be happy, Mrs Jani. The devil sharpens a woman's tongue, Jani, hasn't anybody told you that?'

'Well, I don't think I'd put it in quite such dramatic terms, but she wasn't best pleased. You know the sort of thing – 'get out of the house' ... 'now'.'

Jani's voice began to falter.

'Here come the tears,' said Priest. 'The river of regret is a mighty current and it flows with the meltwater from the glaciers of human hearts, a few more drops won't burst its banks.'

'You're right,' said Jani, wiping his nose, 'blubbing in bars with strangers is no way to go on.'

'Not blubbing in bars won't solve anything either,' said Smoke, who had finished his cigarette. 'Why don't you buy us a drink? We like your story.'

*   *   *

Clara , tired after her shift, pulled into the bus station. She could see a colleague, Bojan, preparing to take the night bus out, the number 14. She parked her bus. There was just one tramp aboard, sleeping across the back seats. She grabbed him by the scruff of the neck, yanked him to the door, and let him drop down the steps and onto the ground. He stumbled off without saying a word, without looking back. Clara locked her bus up and joined Bojan at the window to his cab.

'I shouldn't go home on a bus,' joked Clara. 'I should have a taxi, like a prostitute.'

Bojan laughed,

'Prostitutes only have cabs when they are working,' he said. 'When they travel to work they commute, just like everybody else.'

WEDNESDAY, OCTOBER 2ND

It is clear that an issue such as this must be considered from all angles. Apart from economic and social factors there are other questions: environmental, cultural, engineering and logistical, to name but four. But the major factor, however, is the need to develop so that the system is equal to and compatible with all those around. Trains should connect with busses and cars should be discouraged from filling up the city centre. An integrated transport system, as I have said, is an essential component of modern life. In our case we should strike a balance between building more roads for more and more cars to use, thus enabling people to transport themselves and not building roads so that road transport remains slow and inefficient thus encouraging people not to waste time travelling, which would have bonus effects on the environment.'

Niko put his pen down and looked at the clock. It was three thirty in the morning. Laura had gone two hours earlier. It had taken an hour to straighten out the living room and kitchen. He felt that his essay, eight pages of slightly bigger than usual handwriting, should do the trick. It certainly looked like an essay. He decided not to re-read it all. Doubtless there would be stylistic cracks and the lack of data other than his own personal experiences of transport systems, plus a few uncheckable and made up facts (for example he claimed that Odessa has the fourteenth most integrated transport system in the Black Sea area and that Slovenia had an Integration Index – as defined by the World Bank - of 4.273) did not resonate with credibility. Nonetheless, given the soup making and sex, he felt his work wasn't too bad. At least he had something. Something, to optimistic Niko, was always better than nothing.

*　*　*

At four AM a tear fell from a bridge into the river below. The person whose tear it was saw the tiny blob just before it disappeared into

23

the black water. A beam of light from a headlight struck its surface and made it flash.

In another place, on the opposite side of the world, someone who was sleeping in the day time dreamed about a tear falling from a bridge into a river at night, flashing in headlights. Whose tear it was, where the river might be found and to what sea it flowed to were not part of the dream.

*   *   *

Finally, as the first workers began to emerge from the darkness for the early shifts on the industrial estate, Gregor finished surveying the observations of the previous day. He closed his eyes for a short time. The moon, he thought, as it set behind the jagged outline of the city's South Eastern suburbs, looked pink, like a giant peach.

*   *   *

Very soon Gregor was standing at the door of the shop holding his free newspaper, his free pencil and his free notepad. Karen had insisted that he should not pay for them, after the incident with the change the morning before. Gregor was still out of pocket but he could not be persuaded to accept his change or a free two litre bottle of mineral water and a free four year old jar of capers in kind. He didn't want either. But the note pad, he thought, might be handy. He walked a few steps and then opened the pad and wrote something in it with his new pencil. He did this to demonstrate to Karen, who had touched him with her thoughtfulness, that her present was already proving useful.

'Investigation: first step – define the crime,' he chewed the end of his pencil as he looked at the words. Then he stuffed the pencil and his notepad into his jacket pocket. With a polite wave back at the shop front, he strode off, trying to suggest that the gifts had made him more purposeful than usual, which they hadn't.

Although, as he moved away, at the new speed, Gregor noted, he almost wrote this down in his new notebook with his new pencil, that because he was pretending to feel purposeful he felt more purposeful – about pretending to purposeful. What should he do next to fake purposefulness? The question demanded immediate answers, action.

*   *   *

It was a bright morning, cool and fresh. As yet, the trees were still unshaken, their leaves browning. The town was warm and the smells of summer still rose up from the dust. As Gregor marched briskly towards his office through the open air market, he entered a fog of smells, of coffee, chrysanthemum and hot chestnut fumes, billowing from the stalls and stands of the traders. He slowed as he approached a cafe and, with dying impetus, he flopped onto a flimsy aluminium chair next to one of the curved marble columns of the famous old riverside market building. He could see the butchers within cleaving and shouting; downstairs, in the cool, were the fish; he could just about detect the faint waft of seafood, seeping out from a stone staircase leading underground. Behind him the lazy river gurgled through, almost unnoticed. In front of him was a vegetable stall, at one end was a pile of pumpkins, premature for Halloween, but not for soup, Gregor thought, although he noticed that the stall-holder had hollowed out one snarling face, almost as a joke.

After drinking coffee Gregor moved on, crossing a bridge. In spite of the hiatus in the market, he tried to walk smartly, so as to give the impression that he was not loafing, towards his office. As he wondered about the crimes of the new day and why none of them would be interesting, he failed to notice a black BMW glide slowly past. It stopped a few metres ahead. The window slid down and a man stuck his head out.

'Hey,' he shouted.

Gregor looked around. All he could see were pedestrians, similar to him, warm in their jackets, walking purposefully. Then he noticed the car, the man had stuck his arm through the window and was brandishing a piece of paper.

'Can you tell me where this place is? I've been driving around here for hours,' said the man, who Gregor guessed was in his mid-fifties. His hair was battleship grey and his eyes were blue.

Gregor read the address on the paper. He pointed back down the road and explained that the address did not refer to a building, a house or an office, it was the name of a bridge, not the one he'd just crossed.

'Are you sure?' asked the man. 'I thought it was the name of a club or a cafe?'

Gregor was sure, 'The Fat Dragons' was the name some children gave to one of the bridges over the river, because on each side of the road over the bridge sat four, not particularly frightening looking dragons. Its official name had changed many times: most people just called it the Dragon Bridge, but children, Gregor remembered, called it 'The Fat Dragons', because, as well as not being frightening, the great bronze dragons, chained to substantial stone plinths, were all rather tubby.

Gregor had never liked the dragons. He thought that their self-satisfied, pot-bellied bodies and their jowly faces gave them a smug, petit-bourgeois air. They weren't snarling dragons who would protect the city come hell or high water; they were duplicitous poodle-dragons who seemed to be saying to anyone, from a visiting brush salesman to an invading hoard of horseman: 'come in, take what you like, we'll get the money off you in the end, of that there is no doubt – better still, let's do a deal before anyone gets hurt.'

'I hope this isn't a wind up,' said the man in the car before speeding off.

Gregor walked on. People were getting ruder, or perhaps, rude people were getting smarter cars.

*   *   *

Niko ran across the road; a bus was making for him. The driver had no intention of slowing down. If he was on the bus, Niko had no doubt that the bus would slow down. It would crawl around, a surly hangdog excuse for a piece of machinery, in no hurry to complete its route and link up to other less whimsical networks. It would be a beach donkey of a bus, with a sombrero and holes cut out for its ears to stick up through. Because he wasn't on this bus, it was like a deer, springing around the corner and belting towards the lights with a decidedly integrated joie de vivre. It was the pumpkins Niko was carrying that made running difficult. He was carting three of them, each in its own, taut plastic bag. He had decided to increase the scale of the mashed pumpkin soup situation by producing commercial quantities. He reckoned he could make around seventy four portions with this lot, enough to last until the end of the month. The old man would be pleased.

Clutching the three pumpkins to his chest with both arms, Niko jumped onto the pavement as the bus, with its horn blaring, whizzed past him. Niko shouted 'bastard' as one of the plastic bags burst and a pumpkin rolled out onto the pavement.

An old lady, who had seen the whole thing, tutted. Was it the language she objected to? Niko doubted it: old ladies, in his experience, reserved their choicest swear words for busses. Perhaps it was his swearing at the pumpkin. Old ladies hold pumpkins in quite high esteem.

From the pavement, as he grappled with the pumpkin, Niko smiled up at the lady and apologised. After a second's deliberation she smiled too, nodding her head in the direction of the bus.

'They think they own the road, jumped up little shits.'

*   *   *

'Tosser,' yelled Clara, pressing her foot to the right to floor, 'there are little green men who light up and tell you when to cross the road. And there are places where crossing should occur. You should not simply stroll across a couple lanes of urban traffic and expect to get away with it.'

The bus roared on, none of Clara's passengers took much notice of her little outburst. She watched with satisfaction as the lad in the road flew to the pavement and dropped pumpkins all over the place.

'That'll teach him,' muttered Clara.

One more convert to the gospel of Respect For The Bus; one more pedestrian with an object lesson in crossing the road properly. As she thought about her achievement, Clara made the ancient sign of the bus driver's cult. She stuck her hand out of the window and pointed her middle finger skywards, as her religion dictated.

*   *   *

Gregor paced the floor of his office, his notebook open in his left hand, his pencil in his right. So what was the plot? What crime linked the threads of evidence together? Perhaps there was a more fundamental question: what was the evidence? Was there any evidence at all? Indeed, even if there was evidence: would it be admissible? And if it was, would a majority of the jury see it as compelling after it had been masticated by the lawyers? The briefs could make anything sound like anything else. How many water-tight cases had he watched fall apart at the hands of a 'good' lawyer. The lawyers, Gregor thought, were in with the criminals. Taking the long view, it was the lawyers, not the gang leaders who profited most from crime. But it was worse than that. Gregor was starting to believe that was the main reason why he found it so difficult to investigate crimes. Because once the facts were in the mouths of lawyers, they had a tendency to disintegrate. Stories that once ran purposefully forward towards inevitable and truthful conclusions became infected with madness. Witness statements fell apart, the facts themselves, the certainty that all stories are based on, became questionable and, to Gregor's mind, unintelligible. Then, as the clever lawyers re-built stories so that they satisfied their version of the world, the whole thing turn into jelly. Nothing meant anything – there were no crimes worth investigating because crime stories could no longer be relied upon to make sense.

After an afternoon watching the lawyers turn murderers into victims Gregor sometimes felt, as he walked home, that when he looked at a block of flats, or something substantial, he might be viewing something that just looked like it was a block of flats. It could have been a windmill or a daffodil – that's how the lawyers made him feel. They made him very sceptical about the facts. He sighed as he remembered them – the facts. At the beginning of his career he was almost proud of them. They were real. They were his observations. Now all he could see was everyone else's uncertainty.

Gregor stopped pacing and looked out of his window at the city below. His garden, he used to call it. He harvested crime as a farmer bales straw and, like a productive field, this city never failed. For centuries it had kept guys like him at work, pulling things up and finding things out. Likewise, it had kept fellows like the briefs equally busy, un-finding them out and putting them back. It was a perpetual motion machine, powered by an infinitely renewable, harvestable, environmentally sustainable resource: Trouble. But recently it had been malfunctioning. The jelly was spreading out of its mould because the stories didn't hold together any more. He stared down at the market and watched the pumpkin seller.

Gregor sniffed the air. Up in his fourth floor office, with its heavy wooden shutters, its weighty desk, laden with papers, its ancient and ink stained wooden floor, he felt one step removed from the city. Here the smells of fading summer were overpowered up by the scent of fresh printer paper and formaldehyde. Something was going on, Gregor knew it. Something was stirring beneath the red rooftops that clung to the hill opposite. There were plenty of crimes: rapes, murders, extortions, blackmails, insurance frauds, thefts, beatings, prostitution, drug dealing, but somehow these did not merit Gregor's attention. They were entirely run-of–the-mill shenanigans with no real significance. This time, Gregor's infallible nose told him, it was different. He sniffed. As if tasting the idea. It was big, very big; so big that, for weeks now, he had been unable to respond to any small-scale crimes at all. It was as if everyone was involved. Gregor sniffed again, inhaling more deeply. He felt as if he was on the verge of a great discovery, something that would change the course of his life completely. This big thing, this enormous crime, Gregor was beginning to feel, was everywhere, and yet, it wouldn't reveal itself. He'd never come across one like it before.

Gregor exhaled, it was no good, the great discovery eluded even his attuned nose for a plot. He glanced down at his notebook. He couldn't 'define the crime' but he could sense it – massive, all engulfing, implicating everyone. Alright so there was no smell, nothing for him to sniff, but there was an aperitif of a smell, he just knew it. He sat at his desk and began to scribble in the book. One way, he reasoned, to find a way in, might be to contact as many criminals as he could think of and simply test their mettle. He could eliminate many possibilities by doing this. But there was a problem – even his chief suspects weren't behaving suspiciously.

The Beidecker Twins, for example: although dangerous, the German arsonists were not in town. They were, he believed, operating out of Hamburg, burning real estate for the financial services sector. Dr Ziff, another notorious villain from the University Hospital, was an accomplished murderer and a surgeon.

Because of his high status, nobody had been able to lay a finger on him. Gregor knew that as well as heart bypasses, he also did disconnections - if his backers were wealthy enough. But Ziff was no agent of widespread angst, he was actually very orderly and often the individuals who he did pull the plug on were themselves men and women with a good deal of blood on their hands. Ziff was a kind of expensive and unlicensed cleaner. He wasn't going to rock the boat. Gregor wrote more names down in his book. Layla Sarapoglu, he recalled, had taken up residence near Lake Bled where she conned new arrivals with her fictitious real estate frauds: the market in this town, she had explained, was no longer capable of rendering her increasingly grandiose schemes plausible.

None of the old names fitted. Not one of them had the power to really disrupt things. It seemed to Gregor that all of the agencies of order, both legal and illegal, in one way or other, failed to spot something. And now a great hand was stifling everything, turning even his best ideas into hopeless, tangential ramblings. Something, Gregor, realised, had seized control, but what was it? More to the point, who was it? Who had created this debilitating numbness that infected his head? Who had transformed things happening into nothing happening? Why did he feel so sad? Who could do such a thing? Who would want to do such a thing? Gregor lifted his eyes from his note-pad and looked out at the hillside opposite, with the castle on the top. There was a weed in his garden of human activity - something very unsavoury indeed. Gregor glanced at the books lining the walls of his office – annoyingly they weren't full of criminals' records, they were books on science: mainly biology, botany and taxonomy. He made a mental note to ask someone to get rid of them.

FRIDAY, OCTOBER 4TH

The hunting lodge was a stone box about three paces square with a tiny window high up in one of the walls. The roof was made of wooden beams and turfs and the walls were un-plastered. The floor was compacted earth which went soft when it rained. A heavy man unscrewed more wick and read his correspondence. The official letters looked yellow in the light of the oil lamp.

'Dear Sir,

Thank you for your application to register the name Dormouse Master as a trade mark, filed on the 18th January. An examination has been carried out. The trade mark has been found to be objectionable under Section 18 of the Intellectual Property Act, 1956, on the grounds that it is considered descriptive of the services you offer, being: dormouse-hunting services and the provision of cooked dormice for consumption in restaurants and catering establishments. A search has been carried out and there have been found to be no other applications or registration in the name of Dormouse Master, consequently there is no objection under Section 97(b) of the Intellectual Property Act 1956 on the grounds of conflicting source intimation.

The additional information, plus exhibits, describing your route to the 'discovery' of your name, are noted. For the sake of clarity, and to avoid confusion at a later stage, your submissions have been recorded as:

1/ a pencil drawing of what appears to be a stone hut

2/ a pencil drawing of a vase in a window

3/ a photograph of The Harvest restaurant

4/ a page of hand-written notes stating that you have plied your trade in the forest surrounding the suburbs for a little under forty years; that you were taught how to hunt dormice by a woodsman who said he could trace his lineage back to the time of the Mongol invasions; that your interest in protecting your name as a trade mark has grown in recent years. You are at pains to point out that, normally speaking, you find words, either written or spoken, a poor substitute for experience. In days gone by, when you felt like considering, for example, a tree, you would simply find one. You wouldn't attempt to capture it on paper. Abstract nouns, you believe, are particularly unhelpful. Your application to register Dormouse Master as a trade mark is not inspired by a desire to own words, which you believe have a life of their own, a fact generally overlooked by users of words. Rather, you see your application as defensive – if you like a pre-emptive strike – against other word-users, some commercial, some more poetic, who you believe are seeking to enclose language and therefore curtail access to it through a process of annexation, in the cases of businesses for financial gain and, in the instance of the poets, for narcissistic purposes.

These points are duly noted but have no relevance to the case at hand.

If you disagree with this decision you are entitled to appeal, providing notification is filed within thirty eight days of the date of this letter. Thank you for expressing an interest in registering your mark. You are reminded that application fees are non-refundable.

Yours faithfully,

Mr M Frayling.'

The man bent down. He piled a couple of dormouse traps on top of one another and sat on them. He began to read the next letter, his heavy-lidded eyes traversing the rows of words in a careful, lugubrious, way. He mouthed the sounds as he read them.

'Dear Sir,

Thank you for your letter of the 13th May, querying the objection raised against your application to register the mark Dormouse Master as a trade mark. I have considered your arguments against this decision, but am not moved to waive the objection. A trade mark should, according to the Intellectual Property Act, 1956, identify a trader's goods or services; it should have what is called 'an inherent potential to be construed imaginatively', which, in layman's terms, means that it must be a creative, fanciful, statement, not 'an ordinary observation of known and extant phenomena' or an 'O, O' as they are often referred to. Regardless of the fact that you are, as you claim, the last practising professional dormouse hunter in the country, there is still a strong possibility that your mark will be seen by the public as descriptive of your services and not indicative of you as a freestanding creatively identified source of cooked and raw dormice and provider of dormouse hunting expertise. Should any competitor wish to describe themselves as a Dormouse Master, your registration would prevent them. Clearly this would represent an unreasonable enclosure of language, forcing your competitors to describe themselves in less appropriate ways.

Finally, I note the additional submissions filed in conjunction with your letter: Annex B, a drawing of a dormouse trap; Annex C, a drawing of a string of one dozen dead dormice and, at Annex D, a further explanation of your views. For the purposes of clarity, your analysis at Annex D, entitled 'Why Words, Particularly Abstractions, Are Not Reliable' is summarised here.

Ten years ago, when a customer called at the lodge to find out why you had not delivered a batch of mice, he was horrified to find you on the point of death. You, the self-styled Dormouse Master, lay motionless on the floor of your hunting lodge, with your arm outstretched towards a glass of water perched on the high window ledge. When you recovered, after your customer had handed you the drink, you were able to explain what you were doing. You told him that you had not drunk for four days so that you could feel what it was like to feel thirst, in order to assess the meaning of the words we normally associate with acute water deprivation, as part of your general enquiry into the limitations of description. When, eventually, you decided that you really were dying, after several false alarms (which are detailed at length on pages 7-17 of Annex D), you discovered that you could no longer stand up to reach the water which you had carefully prepared beforehand, leaving it in a glass on the windowsill. As you lay on the floor, contemplating the gravity of your mistake, you realised that your suspicions regarding descriptive terms were well founded, although it is noted that you regret ever having thought up the experiment in the first place. As far as you, the self-styled Dormouse Master were concerned, the single most important word you could find to describe the sensation of dying of thirst is: 'embarrassment'. The meaning of this word is entirely dependent on the unique context in which you found yourself, dying on the floor, a victim of your own ridiculous experiment. Most people would never associate 'embarrassment' with thirst. You conclude that experience is unique and descriptions are not reliable and are always best ignored, in favour of direct, personal experience.

You argue that my understanding of your title is prejudiced by a failure to empathise and imagine accurately, and that, because of this, my refutation of your trade mark application is, itself, unreliable.

I am now formally rejecting this application. It is well established in case law that recourse to metaphysical arguments and 'deliberate semantic ambiguation' [See Civil Court Proceedings Schiff v Scheriff CCP – 4.67.S] is an unhelpful aspect of legal actions regarding trade marks and other semantic rights. At best, this line of argument can be seen as procrastination, at worst it is professional filibustering which is, itself, a punishable crime under the Civil Code (Jenx v Conrad – TMC 76.5). Your submissions are, however, duly noted.

If you disagree with this view, I remind you of your right to appeal this decision through the Court of Industrial Disputes.

Yours faithfully,

Mr M Frayling.'

Slowly the man moved that page from the top of the pile, to the bottom. His fat, earthy fingers held the next leaf.

'Dear Sir,

Thank you for your letter of the 25th June. I must re-emphasise the counterargument to your claim. Your statement that dormouse hunting is unlikely to revive in popularity, given the modern public's squeamish attitude to the consumption of spit roast dormice, is legally inadmissible. The fact that this dish, after several thousand year's existence as a nutritious meaty snack, is being replaced by the hot dog and the hamburger, not to mention vegetarian options, has nothing to do with the meaning of your proposed trade name. Similarly, the fact that nobody would want to become a dormouse hunter in this day and age has no relevance. In law, the possibility of a boom in dormouse hunting is viewed as likely as any other market upturn. If there are no competitors, then potential competitors must be considered, and it is these potentials I am seeking to protect. The evidence you supply clearly shows that you are recognised as the Dormouse Master and that you ply your trade alone. Indeed, you would appear to be something of an anachronism, moving daily from the city like some medieval journeyman. Nonetheless, notwithstanding the arguable uniqueness of your occupation, the possibility that a general revival in the business of dormouse trapping might occur and that other dormouse hunters might seek to benefit from ordinary application of known and extant behaviour, namely, their practice of dormouse hunting and being masters of it, cannot be ignored.

It is also noted that a further submission, at Appendix A, a menu from a popular restaurant in the centre of town has been submitted. For clarity, sections of the menu have been underlined and circled in pencil. These are as follows:

'Starters

Traditional Roast Dormouse – a favourite since Roman times.

Caught using sustainable techniques by our very own dormouse master huntsman.'

You note that when you, the self-styled Dormouse Master, read the menu, you realised why your strategy of avoiding descriptions, words in general, was fraught with danger. Descriptions, you believe, are not merely misleading, they can be like mouse traps, holding living language in cages until the words die. Because everybody else does not subscribe to this view, you now allege that the enclosed, dead language, has developed a power of its own, a commercial one. Moreover, the menu submitted at Appendix A, shows that although you believe words are shifty in character and hard to pin down, other people, shifty characters in themselves, take the opposite view, regarding them as unambiguously meaningful and referring to truth which is held in place by immutable definitions. In short: although you do not believe in the specific meaning of words, you concede that everybody else does. With legal affirmation and dictionary order you allege that this 'cocktail of credulity' (I paraphrase your arguments) has now become the lingua franca of our day and that, through commercialisation and through trade mark registration the stability of words is being concretised by big business interests. Now, you say, you are required to act as if you believed in their veracity, although I understand that, at heart, your original inclination remains intact – that words don't mean much. In this way, you conclude, words in general, and trade marks in particular, are turning into iron bars which can't be broken by free spirited huntsmen such as yourself. Given the menu, and the, albeit passing, reference to the name by which you style yourself (although I note, do not capitalise, which is the usual practice with names), you wish to register the name Dormouse Master as your trade mark, not because you wish to enclose it, but because you want (perversely in my view) to keep it free for others to use, because you see yourself as an 'other'.

I hope this summary adequately describes your views, which, since it has already been rejected (see my official letter of 24th May) remains rejected.

If you disagree with this view, then I remind you of your right to appeal the decision through the Court of Industrial Disputes.

You have 5 days to file an appeal.

Yours faithfully,

Mr M Frayling.'

The Dormouse Master placed the letter at the back of the pile. He had come full circle. He stood up and clomped across the room. A small pile of dormice lay next to a rusty hook in one corner, a rather muddy pile of legal books and papers lay on the ground in another. He stooped to the floor and picked up a spade, his brass stick, some twine and a few other tools and stepped out into the forest.

'A beer please,' said Jani, trying not to move his eyes too much.

'I'm surprised to see you in here,' a familiar voice surprised him. He turned his head slowly.

'My God, it's you.'

Priest sipped his gin, then sniffed his cigar, then scratched his beard.

'You look dreadful,' he said. 'It's Priest, by the way.'

'What happened to me?' asked Jani.

'Search me,' said Smoke. 'You were making for the bridge – we thought you were going to top yourself.'

'Well thanks for stopping me.'

'The last thing you said was that you wanted to be alone. In the mood you were in you wouldn't have thanked us for coming with you and saving your life.'

'You were pretty bad,' nodded Priest, 'suicidal.'

'Yes but I would now, wouldn't I?' said Jani. 'Feeling suicidal and walking to the bridge isn't like going for a game of tennis. And think, I'd be thanking you like mad now, for saving my life and helping go back to my wife to try and sort things out.'

'Which is exactly what you're are doing. You are going back, I take it,' said Priest.

Jani nodded.

'So thank us.'

Jani was incredulous.

'But you nearly killed me – or at least you nearly let me kill myself.'

'Nobody ever throws themselves off the bridge – at least nobody from this bar does. It's too jolly in here,' said Smoke.

'I'm not thanking you. I could have died last night.'

'But you didn't, my friend,' said Priest. 'You didn't and you've had a terrible day and now you've got a hangover and you're here with us. We're here to listen, you should thank us for that.'

Jani was too tired to argue. He filled his mouth with lager. It felt like a jellyfish. He kept his lips tightly shut and swallowed.

'I thought I'd try a hair of the dog,' said Jani, unsteadily.

'You should go home now. Apologise, she'll forgive you,' said Priest.

'She won't,' said Jani.

'She can't if you don't.'

'He's right,' said another voice. It was the quiet fat man.

'Wisdom,' said Priest by way of introduction. 'He doesn't say much.'

'Go home,' said Smoke. 'You've been a welcome guest but... if you hang around here too long, you might find yourself in real trouble.'

'And you look dreadful,' said Priest. 'You make the place look untidy.'

*　*　*

The Fat Dragons, as the children called the big bridge over the river, dipped her feet in the water like a Rubenesque model stepping into a bath. She was a trifle ostentatious, with her chained dragons – jewellery in the bath! She was pale and curvaceous and she was not without her admirers. Once again the traffic was subsiding. The willow trees along the waterfront shivered as the sun disappeared behind the mountains. The days were still warm but, by night, cold could be felt scuttling down into the streets and onto the water. The water was getting chilly.

Two shadowy people were sitting in the front seats of a BMW parked next to one of the fat dragons guarding the bridge. They were not thinking about bathing. They were arguing in the dusk. They had been at it in there all day. The windows were all steamed up.

SUNDAY, OCTOBER 6TH

Buses permitting, Clara would often take herself off to a disused airfield on the outskirts of town, to a car boot sale. Occasionally, she and a friend would set up a stall and sell all sorts of rubbish. They never made any money because they invariably spent their profits on different rubbish from other traders nearby. This Sunday Clara walked through the ranks of bric-a-brac free of responsibility – her son was with his father, her friend was entertaining guests. She had time to peruse the market at her leisure. She was looking for something specific: a fold down kitchen table, the type that screws into the wall so as to free up space. Clara's flat was fifty years old. Its interconnecting door fittings still clicked with precision but, in spite of the good hinges and high standard of installation, the kitchen table was detaching itself from the wall and the unscratchable surface was parting from the plywood top.

Clara's new pram was a three wheeled affair which she'd bought from a man who had spread phone chargers and computer components over a tartan blanket. Now she used the pram as a shopping trolley: in it she had already gathered an old Binatone transistor radio (for the bathroom) and a copper bottomed frying pan, which someone had been using as a container for second hand golf balls. She joggled over the weedy concrete, waving at the traders she recognised, showing off her saucepan. It was always so friendly there. The aerodrome car boot sale lifted Clara's spirits. There was something for everyone. The game was to find it late in the day, just when the store holders were thinking about giving up. At that time, it was a buyer's market.

Clara stopped near the old hangar. Inside, coffee and tea were available. She stood next to an old mustard coloured Volvo DL 245 and checked her change – she couldn't decide whether she wanted a cup of stewed tea or not. She sniffed the air as if, like a bee, she'd been on the trail of something for some time. It wasn't tea that she wanted. For Clara, the scent of moth balls was irresistible. She found herself pulled by naphthalene and camphor to the boot of the old estate car. There was some good stuff there: French antique chairs, a Persian rug, a Hungarian stove, Venetian glass and, presiding over the rubble with clasped hands and a jumpy look on her long face, an intelligent looking woman in her early forties. Clara asked the woman how much she was charging for a small oil painting of mountains. The woman spoke quietly. The price was ridiculously low, not much more than the tea. Clara asked about a glass vase – it was also too cheap. She glanced again at the woman, scrutinising her in the same way as she considered pots and pans. Clara had never seen the woman, or her car, in the market before. She concluded that something had gone wrong to bring her in; she clearly found the experience of selling her prize possessions demeaning. Clara asked about the chairs. The woman, wilting into her woollen coat, once again chose a ridiculously low price.

'Your stuff is too cheap,' said Clara.

'Is it?' said the lady. 'I'm sorry.'

'Would you like me to price it for you?' asked Clara. 'But you must promise not to sell it today. It's too late. Come back next week and make a fresh start.'

The Volvo lady looked embarrassed: she nodded. Together she and Clara spent half an hour going through all the items. In the end Clara worked out that the whole lot was worth hundreds – at car boot morning market prices. It was probably worth thousands at antiques shop prices and the lady assured her that there was tons more of it home. When they finished the stock-take the woman thanked Clara and hugged her. She felt spindly and delicate in Clara's arms. Clara couldn't understand how such a person could arrive at the market – apparently completely unaware of the value of good stuff. The woman, sensing Clara's question, answered it. She told Clara that she was the only daughter of a judge. She had trained as a violinist and had never really got involved with 'money' or, indeed, 'things'. Bad luck had crashed into her family over the past few weeks. Her father had been called into hospital for a routine operation on his knee. He had died of complications – a heart attack whilst he was undergoing surgery. Then she had been informed of the enormous debts he had run up. Although he had been a frugal man who had driven the same car for the as long as she could remember, the life he shared with her was just a side show in his. In his other life, or lives, her father had been reckless and extravagant. She'd been given a matter of days to pay his bills. She didn't know what to do.

Before moving on, Clara told the Volvo lady to double the prices of her antiques. She let the worried woman into a secret – rich people don't want bargains, they want to stand out. If she wanted to make serious money, she should charge at least twice what the furniture would be worth in the most expensive antique shop. Clara looked at the car. She tapped the woman on the shoulder.

'You know what that is?' said Clara.

'We used to go on holidays in it,' said the woman. 'When my mother was alive.'

'Not any more,' said Clara, writing a big number down on a piece of paper. 'It's a classic. Trust me. I drive busses.'

Clara pushed her pram towards the entrance to the airfield, where the bumpy slabs of old concrete join the smooth, bituminous carriageway of the main road. As she approached the main entrance Clara was forced to slow down. The crowds of people strolling in and out, eating from cartons, drinking from plastic cups, carrying purchases and belongings, milling around like mullet at the entrance to a muddy harbour, forced Clara to skirt the fringe. Still aware of the fact that she hadn't found a new collapsible table, she kept her eye on the remaining stalls as she rolled towards the exit.

One stall, the last one, with its back to a thin hedge, the boundary between the road and the airfield, caught Clara's eye. She cast a cursory eye across the table – it was covered in junk, old light bulbs, children's notebooks, well-worn wallets. On the ground, next to the table were shoes: second hand, hard-worn, steel toe capped boots, gum boots, stilettos, slippers.

Clara found herself working her way along a coat rail opposite the footwear. She rummaged her hands between the garments. It was almost as if she was looking for something, or as if she knew that there was something to be found. She stopped searching suddenly. Hanging in the middle of the rack of fraying denim jackets, workman's overalls and kagools, was a black leather coat. Clara pulled the coat out. It was double folded on its hanger and as Clara she held it up it unfurled like a long, black flag. It almost touched the ground. It was beautifully made, lined with black silk, with invisible, tightly sewn seams and rippling folds. The leather felt light to the touch, yet the coat was weighty and strong. Clara had finally discovered the thing that she didn't know she was looking for. She checked the label – 'Zucca'. She smiled, a 'Zucca' coat eh? She'd never heard of them – but she was right about one thing – it was Italian.

A safe distance away from the airfield Clara stopped wheeling the pram and picked up the coat. She pushed her face into it and inhaled. It smelt of perfume, leather polish and tobacco. The next time that tart caught her bus, Clara would be able to able to tell her not to smoke. Because the evidence proved that she was not such a good tart after all – working in the Tivoli (of all places) and selling her best assets at the car booter: neither of these things were in the slightest bit cool. She was the cool one now.

MONDAY, OCTOBER 7TH

'What the hell do you think you've been doing?' she shouted, gesticulating around the kitchen. 'The whole place is covered in pumpkin. Everywhere pumpkin! You've even got it in the bathroom sink.'

'I'm going to freeze it,' said Niko.

'We haven't got a freezer,' she said. 'And anyway, he only eats small amounts at any given time. You've got enough pumpkin soup here to last a month.'

'Two and a half, actually,' said Niko. 'Laura's got a freezer. I'm going to put it in empty pickle jars and freeze them. That way we'll have small meals for him whenever he wants.'

'And where are your pickle jars pots?'

'We've all got to eat a lot of pickle for a couple of days. It's getting colder now, we can keep the soup outside in the nights, it won't go off.'

Niko's mother, a well-presented manager in a red suit, began to clear up the kitchen. She'd called in on the way to work. She hadn't expected things to have drifted so far. Niko conceded that the quantities of pumpkin he had been dealing meant that most of the utensils in the kitchen had been pressed into service. He agreed that the pumpkin splattered on the walls, floor and windows was slippery, unhygienic and unsightly. But he would not accept the argument that his basic plan was flawed. What were they going to feed the old man when the pumpkin season came to an end? His mother had not thought about that.

'The truth is,' said Niko. 'You don't care. I'm the one who looks after him. You just float in here every now and again wringing your hands saying how unfair it is.'

'That's not fair,' said Niko's mother, as she sniffed a saucepan encrusted with dry pumpkin juice.

'What else do you do?' asked Niko.

'Pay,' said his mother. 'I pay.'

'Oh big deal, with whose money? With that tosser of a boy friend's money – not yours.'

'He's my partner. He's very kind and you'd do well to watch your lip.'

'Look, I'm the one that lives here. I'm the one that looks after him. Why don't you just go in there, wring your hands a bit more and piss off? It'll make you feel better.'

'Not until I've cleaned this mess up,' said Niko's mother, producing a pair of yellow rubber gloves from her red handbag. 'Then I suppose we'd better find something to put all this soup into.'

Niko left the kitchen, taking care not slip on the Lino.

* * *

Out in the forest it was dark. It was always dark. It was dark in the day time and even darker in the night. There was a crackle, it sounded like a twig breaking under a footfall, in fact, it was the sound of the Dormouse Master opening a letter. He stepped into a shaft of sunlight penetrating the canopy and read.

'Dear Sir,

Regarding you application to register the words Dormouse Master as a trade mark, a date for your case to be heard has been arranged. You are required to attend the court of Industrial Property on October 21 at 12.30pm. The hearing will be held in Main Court Room No1. Non-attendance will result in forfeiture of all rights.

Yours faithfully,

Mr M Frayling.

PS It is extremely unusual for me to offer advice to parties appealing my own decisions. However, in your case, because you claim not to require formal legal representation and yet clearly have little grasp of the full subtlety of regulatory law and the long and illuminating case histories most advocates consider essential, I will offer you one suggestion. You would do well to note that, on considering Annex D in your submission of the 13th May, I said in my letter of 1st June that I believed that its implication (namely, that all words, particularly when used to describe events [in this case your own near death experience] are inherently unreliable because of the subjectivity of their users) is likely to fall within the ambit of a 'deliberate semantic ambiguation' as defined in law, which, of itself, is a criminal offence. The key test in matters of DSA, as it is known, is whether a party knowingly resorts to deliberate semantic ambiguation. I must warn you that, since you are now aware of this possibility, further recourse to the 'semantic argument', will result in in counteractive criminal proceedings for the reasons previously stated. Because you are now aware of the consequences of your thinking, you are responsible, whereas before, you were merely ignorant. You may be familiar with the old saying: 'a bear, once awake, doesn't sleep until summer is over.'

The Dormouse Master arose from his tree stump. He shoved the paper into his pocket and walked away, towards a set of traps. To reach them he had to cross the top of a steeply sloping field. From this vantage point it was possible to look down a valley and see most of the city spread out in the distance like a map. Years ago the Dormouse Master used to bring customers to this spot; they enjoyed trying to find their houses in the distant streets below. From here the Dormouse Master could also see a track winding from his hunting lodge, through the woods, down to the field and on until it joined a tiny road. On warm, bright days this track would get blocked with cars belonging to people from town, out for a walk in the woods or even a picnic. Since today was a sunny one, there were already few cars there, shining in the glowing landscape. Amongst them was a black BMW.

*   *   *

'You're pathetic,' said the woman.

The man reached for the woman's hand but she drew it away with a hiss. Her jaw was strong. She was striking, like a movie star or one of those pre-Raphaelite lookers.

'Don't touch me,' she said, pushing her voluminous auburn hair back into place.

'Sorry,' said the man. He was a little older, in his early fifties. He looked tired and grimy. He had been wearing the same suit for three days. He thumped the dashboard with his hands.

'I didn't mean that.'

'What didn't you mean?' asked the woman, her eyes flashing. 'Which bit of all of the things didn't you mean?'

The man leant back into his seat. He sighed, casting his eye over the field and the city below. He pushed his hand through his silver hair, affecting an air of confidence.

'That we should take this opportunity to get re-acquainted. I didn't mean that, I wasn't thinking straight.'

The man took the woman's hand again. This time she watched it as if it wasn't hers.

'How could you think about sex at a time like this?' asked the woman.

'Quite easily, to be honest. You're very sexy - I'm very stressed. I feel horny when I get stressed. Politics is like that – it's why politicians sleep around so much. We're all stressed to fuck... You've got wonderful breasts, I don't think I can find the words to describe how alluring I find the way you arrange them.'

The woman watched a man, probably a farmer, skirting the edge of the field, where the forest began.

'This doesn't make me feel horny,' she said. 'It makes me angry. Why the fuck do you want to describe my breasts?'

'I'm being affectionate. We've been driving around the place for days now. We don't need to argue all the time.'

She pulled her hand away.

'Let's get one thing straight. This is your fault. If the facts ever come out I will be able to walk away. You will be sent to prison. I am here because I have to be. It's my job. For the time being I have no option but to support you. But let me tell you this, I want you to know that I think everything you have done so far has been, shallow, infantile and dangerous. You clearly do not have the intelligence to get yourself out of this mess, so from now on you must listen to me.

You don't try to grab my hand when you're feeling sorry for yourself and you stop looking at my tits when I'm speaking.'

The man tried not to look at the woman's breasts. She was wearing a dress, it wasn't so big. It was colourful – flowers, perhaps: big blue, purple and yellow ones.

'We're talking about a murder here. How can you be so pathetic? 'I'm not being pathetic. It's just that we've been together for days. I'm under pressure. I'm bound to notice aren't? You make a big enough deal of them.'

'We've been together for a lot longer than three days, Slabo. I became your private secretary eight years ago. In case you have forgotten you saw these breasts quite regularly then. There are no surprises in this dress.'

Slabo stared at the dress. He disagreed. Perhaps that was what he was finding so difficult to articulate: the dress' potential for surprises.

'That was only because you wanted the job.'

'You gave me the job because I wanted to fuck you. I wanted to fuck you to get the job. What's wrong with that? I'm not perfect. You're not perfect. Nobody's perfect. And stop looking so bloody hangdog. This is not some misdemeanour that can be overcome with apologies and long faces. This is murder.'

Slabo's face changed. His eyes bulged. His voice turned from water to steam.

'Don't you fucking lecture me you stupid fucking bitch. If you want you can just get out of the car, I'll fix this on my own. I don't need you. You are as disposable as that stupid fucking whore.'

'Is that a threat? Are you going to have me killed too?'

'That's one job I might like to do myself.'

'What, bury me in the woods, here?'

'Exactly.'

'What about the bloke up on the hill?'

'What bloke, what hill?'

The woman pointed across the field at the Dormouse Master, trudging towards them.

'You'll have to murder him too. And those people walking the paths below him. And the other guy. There's a principle here, Slabo, you cannot kill your way out of death. You have to be more subtle.'

What the fuck is that supposed to mean?' demanded Slabo.

'You have to move death away altogether. You have to disassociate yourself from it. In your case that means re-writing history.'

'It happened didn't it? We can't deny that. You can't re-write history.'

'A politician who says he can't rewrite history. Give me a break. When you left university you were a radical. You hated the communists because they sold out. Now you are a member of the most exclusive gym in town, you have a houseboat on the lake and you play golf on Sundays. Things change. History is just the story of how people want their pasts to look. Today, there are only stories, Slabo. It's singularly easy, nobody really believes in anything, all we have to do is make up a really convincing story for ourselves, make sure it's a good one and stick to it. It will become the truth. It will become the explanation for the tragic death of a whore who had delusions of grandeur and nothing to do with you.'

'An alibi, I've got one of those,' growled Slabo. 'I was in a meeting.'

'Alibis are pot boilers for lawyers. History is for everyone. I'm talking about the total reinvention of your character, your beliefs, and your values. Once you've sorted that lot out, the business of where you were at any particular moment will seem utterly trivial. You will be able to brush things aside because the whole idea of what is, what was, what isn't and what wasn't will become a blur, dependent on your story. You get me?'

Slabo nodded, stroking his chin as he watched the field.

'So who am I?'

'You'll have to decide, it shouldn't be so difficult, you're an opinion former. I'll take you back to the office. You look dreadful.'

* * *

On the way home from work, Gregor returned to Karen's shop to buy his evening paper. Two men outside were installing an iron grille over the windows. Inside Karen busied herself hanging Halloween trimmings up from her shelves skeletons, witches' hats and orange balloons which looked like pumpkins. She whispered to Gregor as she squeezed past him to reach the till.

'I don't feel safe anymore. I expect you feel the same, walking back from the university on these chilly evenings. We're all potential victims you know.'

THURSDAY, OCTOBER 10TH

'The Journal of Slabo _____, Minister for Culture,

For the first time in my political career, I have failed to keep my records up to date. I have been attending to an unfortunate business. I returned to my office in town a few days ago and left Ms Vala strict instructions to leave me undisturbed to allow me to reinvent myself. This process has taken more time than I had anticipated. I have resolved to sort this business out for once and for all, and, after taking advice from Ms Vala, who has been a loyal friend and a dedicated civil servant, I feel that it is only right for me to take responsibility for my actions. I have cancelled all my appointments. For one more day I will be absent without leave. However, it is a Thursday afternoon, tomorrow is a Friday, traditionally a slack day, so I have no particular business to cancel. I make a note here, for the record, that were the diary to be full, all meetings would have been cancelled.

My desk is covered with yellow strips of note paper with messages on them for me, left by people visiting my office during my brief absence. This one from the Congress of Small Businesses says that they found my non-appearance at their meeting, 'disappointing'; there are the Norwegians, Frenchmen and people from some petrol company, there is the Minister for Employment, a cabinet meeting, a dinner with the someone from the Dutch royal family, a speech to the Chamber of Commerce, all unattended, all resulting in little yellow stickers on my desk.

None of this matters.

Certainly, I can re-schedule the meetings. I can blame it all on stress or a cold sore or some personal loss. I could say I was getting divorced. But first I would need to speak to my wife and the truth is I haven't seen her for two years – arranging a conversation may be difficult. I see that there are no notices from her on my desk. So I presume she is doing well.

When I began this diary, all those years ago, it was supposed to be a truthful and comprehensive description of everything that happened in my political life – it was both a record and an insurance policy. By recording the facts as they occurred, in the order in which they presented themselves, I had hoped that it would be possible for future historians to see that at any given moment I took the best decision possible. My diary was the defence shield against careless revision. This diary was to be the source which I could use for my memoires and the database historians would access to create their work, accurately. It was also my personal pension fund – because I thought that the diary would always prove me right. After all, it is my diary.

There was, however, another, less magnanimous reason for writing this diary. In politics one inevitably gets shafted. I wanted a record that would grant me the privilege of paying the bastards back. Anyone who backed me into a corner had to bear this record in mind. I made no secret of it. If someone screwed me they were noted in my brown book. I recorded their actions and then, eventually, if they thought it was safe to transform themselves from lamentable toadying arm twisting shits into benevolent day time TV presenters, I would be there with my facts. I recorded as much as I could, because I knew I could not tell precisely what was crucial and what was just chaff at any particular point in time. They say that Napoleon lost the battle of Waterloo because he had haemorrhoids. Who's to say that the attack wasn't triggered off by the same thing that catapulted him to success – his love of artillery. Who's to say that that he didn't spend too much time resting his imperial buttocks on the freezing metal shafts of his beloved cannons and that the very instruments of his success weren't also responsible for his final humiliation at the hands of a ramshackle bunch of Belgians and Englishmen? My aim was to make it so I knew the truth by recording everything, even the number of times I sat on a cannon.

Where was I?

God I'm tired.

I've been in the car for days.

This is what I'm trying to say.

I should have recorded the following events in my journal but, for the first time, I practised a degree of censorship, for my own good, for the following reasons:

number one: it was compromising;

number two: it was a secret;

number three: it wasn't me.

Let me explain. When I go to open an extension to a cake factory or chair a cabinet meeting on infrastructure development I am Slabo, the administrator. I make good decisions. I remember everybody's names: places, faces, addresses, even how countless numbers of very dull people like their coffee: strong, sugary, milky, black, frothy, I could go on. I am an expert at recalling the minute predilections of small, self-interested people when they appear in large rooms. I am an excellent politician. When I am not performing my miracles of memory (I know most almost all my constituents' names), I am another person - a less attentive one. I do not particularly care how you take your coffee and I do not wish to be remembered at all. But I stifle my urge to become environmental. The politician will remember everyone because he wishes, more than anything else in the world, to be remembered. But this other version of me doesn't give a shit, he likes hiding at the back of the room. Which one of these people am I? the disinterested, anonymous one or the fastidious, well known one? It is a good question - they live together: one delighting in the shade afforded by the other who basks in the superfluity of spare light. At first I blamed the anonymous one, not the careful one who writes the diary.

And now, you see, if I am honest, right here, right now, I think that I am neither of those two. How would I be able to pass judgment on those two chaps if I wasn't someone else? Those two behave like a king and like a dog. The dog is always doing bad things. He drinks too much. He sleeps with too many women. He smokes outside the building with a hat drawn low over his face. The other is too good to be true. He is forever dropping coins in beggar's hats and smiling into children's faces, remembering their bloody names. The real me is the third person, the one who has to run between the king and the dog trying to encourage them to work together productively. Perhaps he is the one who has been keeping the secret. He's the one who takes the notes.

A week or so back the two people got mixed up. I mean by this that that the king and the dog both came out together at the same time. They mingled in the way of oil and vinegar, temporarily transforming into French dressing. I mean that at more or less the same time they collaborated and then they behaved badly.

It had been a long day. I had had meetings with all sorts of boring people. They are all recorded in the diary. There was dinner in honour of some general who was retiring and, after that, some of my colleagues and I went into town, for relaxing drinks. The evening wore on, we stayed out quite late. All I said was that it would be a hell of a lot simpler if a certain person was dead. It was not an instruction. It was a late night grumble articulated by these two versions of myself who both seemed to be enjoying each other's company over a drink and who both seemed to want to say something – perhaps one of them just wanted to show off to the other. Neither of them appreciated just how dumb my civil servants were. One of them, a new boy, green behind the ears, anxious to please, listened to the story about a tart I was seeing. I said that I thought that she was going to blackmail me or, worse, simply put me in the newspapers and try to ruin my career. In fact she was a lovely tart. Physically, she reminded me of one of Picasso's alluring but slightly disturbing call girls – eyes pointing in all directions – ears mixed up in her hair. She was completely incapable of organising a serious campaign against me. We'd just had a disagreement, in the Tivoli hotel, of all places. Anyway, the king and the dog betrayed themselves, the idiot acted, the girl died and then the idiot disappeared.

You see how difficult it was to write that. My diary is supposed to be a historical record that will benefit and protect me, not destroy me. To be honest I don't quite know why I am writing this part. I will have to pull out the pages later on. But at the moment, the third version of me wishes to write and neither of the other two is strong enough to object.

I dislike both of my other parts.

I feel tired.

I will never let this document fall into the public domain.

I know I can trust myself to tear this page out and burn it, or maybe even eat it.

Now the dog, the king and the one who brokers the deals

between the two are all in the open. I have just one more question. Who is writing this diary now? I can assure you it is none of those three. As I sit here watching my hand push my pen across the page I know that they are not involved. Now that they have the facts they all agree that this kind of stuff shouldn't go in the diary at all. All they want to do is to go to sleep. No, there is another wakeful one, the one who writes the diary regardless of motivation, who has some kind of death-wish for putting things down on paper. Why doesn't he stop writing? Who is this fourth person? The one whose words you are reading now, the one whose voice you can hear in your head. He, or maybe even she, is the writer, the real me. But when I ask the ringleader to step forward, that fellow is replaced by another and then another. I find a fifth, then a sixth, then a seventh Spartacus. In fact, now that I look, I can see a long, long corridor full of my shadows. They look like a row of winter coats, floating on hangers. I am not number four, or five or six. Every time I think about myself another coat appears.

Perhaps we should proceed in this way: that old one, we'll call him Number Four, is not me, for I can already tell he isn't writing this diary any more either. I will reinvent myself, just as Vala asked. The person you know, the one whose voice you can hear, the person who really is me, the writer of these words will be known, from now on, as Not Number Four. At least we can agree that is definitely true. You now know me by this name, although everybody else calls me, all of my versions, Slabo. Indeed, perhaps, when I was not writing, that is who I was.

Vala thinks the idiot will never talk and that if he does he won't be believed. She thinks I can rebrand myself and rewrite the story for all of us. Vala is wrong. In trying to reinvent myself all I have found is that I'm Not Number Four. What kind of conclusion is that? People will lock me up – not for murder, but for taking the piss. Perhaps the best thing I can do is to stop writing. Maybe if I destroy my journal, then I will become Slabo.'

TUESDAY AND WEDNESDAY, OCTOBER 15TH AND 16TH

In town Clara's bus zipped around its route like a whippet chasing a hare. She stopped at the bottom of Castle Hill. The traffic lights shone like pebbles at the bottom of a crystal clear pool, advertisements sparkled all around in the milky afternoon light. A boy stepped aboard, interrupting Clara's daydream. She recognised him, not knowing where from. It was Niko. He was wearing his best jeans and his leather jacket. He was going to town to meet Laura and some friends at an open air rock concert in the market square.

'Hi,' he said.

'Give me the money and sit down,' said Clara.

'Alright,' said Niko, counting out some cash. 'What's eating you?'

'Nothing,' said Clara. She didn't like the boy.

The boy took his ticket and stepped down the bus.

'Start spreading the news...' Clara sang as she slewed around the corner at the Hotel Tivoli. The tart had disappeared. It was a shame, because she wanted to surprise her.

'Hey!' shouted Niko. 'What the hell do you think you are doing?'

Clara checked her mirror and watched Niko drag himself back to his feet. There was something over-familiar about his indignant tone. She didn't like that. It put her in mind of her ex-husband. He'd started off similar to Niko, handsome, fit looking, bright, funny, a chancer, a blagger, great fun. Clara sighed, Niko was going to grow up into the kind of man she hated; feckless, lazy and irresponsible. She glared at his confident, open face. She wanted to squish him like a head louse before he grew any bigger.

'Sit down and shut up,' she said.

'Look,' said Niko, approaching the front of the bus, 'I don't have to put up with this. I paid my fare. I'm entitled to a comfortable ride.'

With a menacing grin, Clara span her wheel sending the bus slewing around another corner.

'Sorry,' yelled Clara watching Niko clinging to hand rails with both hands.

As he swayed she recognised him. Perhaps it was the manner in which Niko tried to stay on his feet that reminded her of the slouching boy with pumpkins who had ambled across her lane earlier. This kid needed to be taught a lesson. He needed to respect the interior of the bus as well as its external livery. Then, perhaps, he would be more considerate to the women in his life.

*   *   *

It was Janja who left the shop. Not Gregor. Gregor had walked in, noticing the men fixing the iron grille but Janja stepped out, making the same observation but in a different way. The shop was the spot where Gregor left Janja.

She stumbled onto the pavement, blinking - as if a blindfold had been removed from her head. She lurched outwards like a drunk. She'd become so accustomed to Gregor's way of doing things that she couldn't remember how to move her own body. She was acutely aware of her legs. They were heavy and difficult to shift and she was sure that she could sense the blood roaring through them. The legs wouldn't work. She had to consciously organise their walking, stepping with the teetering uncertainty of a new-born calf, waving her arms in the air for balance - like a mad person. She ordered the legs to obey, screwing up her face and snarling like a sergeant major: 'one', 'two' each time a shoe full of blood and bone collided with the concrete. By the time she'd reached the entrance to her apartment block, Janja had taken command, the legs had been pacified and subdued; once again they belonged, more or less, to her.

Janja rested her hand on the cool aluminium door handle pausing to inhale the autumn air. It filled her mouth as if it was food and she was eating it. Gregor seemed to have tuned her senses to suit himself. He was clearly a little deaf, the jingle of Janja's keys made her ears ring; the cold of the handle bit into her fingers, that would be the thick skin. Janja looked back towards the shop, trying to force the moment when she'd stopped being Gregor into her memory. It was disappearing from her mind's eye like a dog's stick in the backwash. She knew it was important to remember because it was unbelievable, she already understood that she had to remember it to keep it true. Karen had handed her the newspaper, Gregor had turned to the door and then she heard Gregor's voice, loud and clear: 'goodbye'. Then she leant on the door and everything changed. The door opened, disgorging her onto the street, unable to walk properly.

Later that night Janja sat at her round, white kitchen table. She read the message she'd just written. She sipped a glass of wine. Janja screwed up the piece of paper and dropped it into the bin. She knew that this was the last time she would do this.

Janja pushed her chair backwards, the legs squeaked on the clean white tiles. She stood, turning and stepping towards the fridge. She opened the fridge. There was only one thing in the fridge - her half-empty bottle of white wine. Janja filled her glass and drank to the end of years of lunacy. It was over. Peter had gone too.

Janja put the bottle down on the table. The fridge leaked its eternal purr. The white wall tiles shone as brightly as they had on the day that they were applied. The glass fruit bowl refracted light from the fluorescent tube above, creating a small example of a rainbow.

Janja moved to the living room. The fabric in there made her feel less edgy. She placed her glass on the wooden coffee table, spilling a drop.

*   *   *

It was some time since Niko had drunk home-brewed beer. He stared through the side of the lemonade bottle he'd just been given.

'Careful you don't stir the sediment up,' said Snap.

Niko searched for the sediment at the bottom. Disappointingly, there wasn't any. He had a bottle of Danube flood-water. He unscrewed the top. There was a plaintive hiss. Something in the bottle had just died.

'Drink it,' said Snap. 'It's great'.

Doubtfully Niko raised the bottle to his lips.

It was not 'great'. But neither was it utterly unpalatable. Then again, it didn't taste like beer. There was a yeasty, peppery quality to the drink. He swilled the liquid around his mouth then pronounced judgement: 'Mesopotamia, 5,000 years BC. Congratulations, this is stone-age lager. You've got 7,000 years before you evolve into decent pint.'

Niko wandered off. It was a cold, moonless, starry evening. A band played on a temporary stage in front of a small crowd. They weren't exactly popular, so there was plenty of space in the market square. Niko ambled to one of the marble columns supporting the meat market roof and watched. He knew the singer, he was an obnoxious economics student called Eric. He was in love with Vita the guitar player. She was in love with herself. She struck a pose and a chord. Eric went down on one knee and held the base of his microphone stand aloft so that the shaft and the mic itself pointed directly up at the castle. It was, Eric thought, a great, gothic, heavy rock position to be in. The castle, the trees, the starlit night, the candle-lit pumpkins with their toothy smiles lined up along the front of the stage, the old skeleton borrowed from the college science lab, all added to the effect. He was The Overlord of Rock. All he needed were some bats.

'Oh, Oh, Oh, Oh, Oh, Oh, Oh, Oh, Oh, Oh, yeeeeaaaa, baby, baby babeeeeeeeeeeeeeey.'

Vita struck another chord, this time turning her back to the audience and arching her back so that everyone could see what a nice arse she had.

'Baby, baby, baby. Yeah,' shrieked Eric.

'I really need you baby,' he moaned.

The drums kicked in and the band launched into one of their own compositions: *'I really need you baby.'*

Sipping his beer, Niko, tried to ignore Eric and Vita. He pushed off his column and wandered through the crowd exchanging pleasantries with his friends. He felt sorry for Eric on stage, playing carboniferous rock as if it had something pertinent to say. If Niko had a band, he knew what he would sing about: integrated transport systems, the possibility of building cheap reliable earthquake proof buildings, health service reforms, songs of international understanding and the need for a responsible banking system. Niko laughed as he imagined track list of his latest album: 'Includes the hit single: 'The Tram Systems of Poland – A Case Study.'

He spotted some of the girls from college gathered around a table where a few students were selling hot mulled wine and burgers. The

ir hands around their plastic glasses as they talked.
rrived they fell silent.

ıı girls,' said Niko.

Eleanor said something to fill in the empty conversation.

'Hi Niko, have you seen Marko and Snap?'

'Snap gave me this,' said Niko, waving his bottle. 'It sucks. Why?'

'I just wondered,' said Eleanor.

'They're here somewhere,' said Niko. 'Where's Laura?'

There was a slight pause, Eleanor and Laura were best friends.

'She said she might not come tonight,' said Eleanor. 'She's got a big essay to write.'

Niko nodded, Laura hadn't mentioned this to him.

'And she's not feeling well,' added Eleanor, offering Niko a glass of wine.

Niko took the glass in his spare hand and joined the girls for a few minutes, thinking that they wanted him to stay. Eleanor introduced him to a new girl, Sabel, she was visiting. They stood and watched 'I really need you baby' until it stopped. Then, since nobody was talking, Niko finished his wine, thanked the girls and moved on. As soon as he had gone the girls resumed their conversations.

Niko found Marko behind the stage negotiating dope prices with a middle aged rocker called Pinkie from the Iguana rehearsal rooms.

* * *

It was two am and Niko was thinking to himself that perhaps the evening had been interesting only because of the absence of a defining event – the 'thing' that happened. Nobody had drunk too much, thrown up, hit anyone, stolen anything, fallen off the stage, electrocuted themselves, slipped into the river, missed their bus, got off with someone's boyfriend or girlfriend, or even just perforated an ear drum. Even the tiresome music had improved, or perhaps the home brew made just made it seem that way. Now he, Marko, Snap and the girl who was visiting college on an exchange were walking home. They made their way along the traffic free road, from the market square to the Fat Dragons. Snap was talking to the stranger, trying to persuade her to relax more. He offered her homebrew and spliffs. But she politely declined. She said she was tired.

They crossed the empty bridge, the boys laughing and shoving each other towards the balustrades, occasionally pausing to watch the black water slither by below. Although they were drunk, they were all pleasant to the girl, occasionally breaking off from their loud and ridiculous chatter to ask polite questions: 'how long was she staying?', 'how was she finding her stay?', 'would she ever come back again for a proper holiday?'

The girl answered as accurately as she could, saying that she was enjoying the first week of her one month visit, that she found everybody very hospitable and that she would definitely be returning for a holiday – but in summer time, because the weather was getting a little cold in the nights.

They reached the other side of the bridge and passed a taxi rank, there were three or four cabs, their drivers standing around smoking and talking. No one had enough money for a cab, so they continued down the road without even bothering to discuss the possibility of hiring one. Just a little further on from the cabs was a parked car, a black BMW, moored by the railings next to the river, shaded from the starlight by a willow tree.

They continued from the centre of town with its concrete offices and stately nineteenth century buildings into the idiosyncratic Riverside suburb. There were no streetlights here, there were no shop fronts throwing light from their signs, no burger bars, kebab shops, twenty four hour Bureaux de change; no night clubs with flashing lights. The river and its tributaries were even darker and idler here. It meandered like a black cat's tail through the bungalows and gingerbread villas. Small streams, old mill races, canals and drainage ditches quartered the streets beneath a starlit spiders' webs of willow branches and telephone cables. Children from the local school had decorated the lower branches of the trees with witches riding broomsticks. They turned silently in the soft breeze, as if they were powered by starlight.

It happened here, on an old hump backed bridge over a ditch. It was the thing that always happens - the event that makes a night memorable. A man appeared from behind a tree.

'Oh shit,' thought Niko recognising the thing.

Instinctively he, Marko and Snap flicked their joints into the water below.

'Hi,' said the man.

'Keep walking', Niko whispered to Sabel.

The man joined them as they hurried away from the bridge. He seemed jumpy, like he was on something.

'Have you got a cigarette?' he asked.

They stopped. Marko and Snap looked at Niko. It should be OK, there were three of them. They guy seemed harmless. Snap produced a smoke and handed it to the man.

'Have you got a light?' he asked.

Snap lit the man's cigarette with his Zippo lighter.

'Thanks,' said the man. 'You got any money?'

Marko, Snap and Niko all started walking, waving goodbye to the nut case. But Sabel, who wasn't so aware of what was going on and how people were communicating, found herself separated from them. She was the wrong side of the man. So as the boys moved off. He was able to block her path.

Niko saw this, he hurried back saying loudly as he held out an arm as if to put it around the girl's shoulders, as if she was his girlfriend and they were together and she really did know what was going on.

'Come on Sabel, it's this way.'

But before Niko could get to Sabel the man pulled a big knife out of his coat pocket. Without thinking, Niko dipped his shoulder and charged into the man. At the same time he yelled at the others to run.

Marko and Snap turned on their heels. Niko, after knocking the man over, scrambled to his feet and sprinted off as fast as he could, assuming Sabel was already well on her way. Niko caught Marko and Snap around the next corner. There was no sign of their assailant. Unfortunately, there was no sign of Sabel either.

Marko poked his head around the corner. He could just about make out two figures in the gloom, by river bank.

'The fucking silly cow didn't run,' he hissed.

Snap looked.

'Fuck,' he said,

Niko looked.

'She probably didn't understand,' said Niko.

'Where the fuck does she come from?' said Marko. 'It's pretty straight forward. What part of 'run' is there not to understand?'

'I dunno, it slows you down, being a visitor.'

They watched as the man pulled Sabel back over the bridge and down towards the river.

'Come back here or she gets it,' he shouted.

Niko looked at the others.

'What are we going to do?' said Marko.

'Well,' said Niko, 'I don't think we can let him kill her.'

Snap considered this for a moment.

'You're going to have to go for the cops. I'll go back,' Niko said.

Marko gave Niko a touching punch on the shoulder before grabbing Snap by the collar and running off down the road. Niko stepped out from behind his corner, crossed back over the bridge and joined the man and girl down on the river bank.

'Where are the others?' asked the man.

'Those two?' said Niko. 'They won't stop running for a month, man. They're history.'

'How much you got?'

Niko was taken aback by this question. He looked at Sabel, her white faced smeared out of shape by the hand crushing her mouth, her brow hair hanging low over the knife at her throat, her blue eyes flashing with confusion.

'Money?' asked Niko. 'Are you for real?'

'Money, of course money,' said the man, tightening his grip.

Niko looked at Sabel.

'It's OK,' he said, trying to reassure her. She didn't look reassured, although she tried to, for the sake of good manners.

Niko began to search through his pockets regretting the fact that he had spent the entire evening drinking home brew in order to save money. If he'd have known he'd end up getting mugged, or having to pay a ransom, he'd have drunk proper beer. But then, again, he thought, if that had happened he would have been genuinely skint and then what would have happened?

'How much do you want?'

'Everything,' said the man.

Niko showed the contents of his pockets to the man. There were a couple of notes, lots of change.

'It's everything. Honestly,' said Niko. 'I'm a geography student.'

'Put it on the grass,' said the man.

Niko put the money on the grass.

'Step well back.'

Niko stepped well back.

He watched the man with his wild, lank hair, a hungry face and the remnants of a suit hanging off his body like a mummy's bindings. He saw the girl, terrified. He wanted to speak, to plead with the man not to kill Sabel. But before he could, the man shoved her towards him. She toppled across the pavement. Niko grabbed her as she gasping for air. The man scooped up the money and vanished. Niko didn't see where he went because the girl was snivelling and whining in shock and she'd thrown herself into his arms.

'It's OK,' said Niko. 'You're OK.'

The rest of the night was predictably bureaucratic. The police showed up first, followed closely by an ambulance. Sabel went to hospital. Niko, Snap and Marko spent the night in a cell. At the hospital, possibly overcome by the verisimilitude of her cultural exchange, Sabel fainted; she didn't come around until the following afternoon.

For everybody, apart from Niko, Sabel, Marko and Snap, the events on the riverbank near the hump back bridge, appeared hazy. There were too many ambiguities. The police didn't believe that the boys didn't have a better story.

'Why did he not take your credit card and force you to make withdrawals from a nearby bank?' they asked.

'You'll have to ask him that,' Niko kept saying. Somehow he felt the police were blaming him for the fact that he had no idea what the motivation of the man was.

'Why didn't Sabel run?' they wondered.

'It's not my responsibility,' said Niko.

It wasn't good enough. The police didn't take kindly to Niko, his story, its motivational gaps, his cocksure demeanour, his friends, his observations. He gave them the impression that he was holding something back, or worse, that he was scratching their procedures against the disorder all around to produce an amusing effect.

Niko and the others were eventually released the following evening, after a visit from his mother's boyfriend, who was a lawyer. He made representations.

'Why did you go back to help the girl?' they had asked, suspiciously.

* * *

Earlier Jani had decided to take his family to the ballet. His wife, her mother (her father had declined the offer – preferring to watch football at home on the TV), his two daughters all had tickets. Jani saw the night out as an important peace offering – a step towards rehabilitation. He had been tempted. He had transgressed. He had done wrong. But isn't ballet supposed to deal with all of that kind of stuff? Don't women love ballet? Isn't that because ballet shows true love and how important it is, even though things can go wrong? Isn't ballet a peace-maker in the war between reality and dreams? Isn't that because the people in ballets jump and leap and curl up and touch? They don't just go on and on at each other with words?

Jani asked himself questions as he watched the dancers bounce across the stage in the awestruck theatre, wiggling his toes to the tunes of The Moscow Ballet's Nutcracker.

The acoustics of the 'modern' concert hall (completed in 1971) were famous. Or perhaps Jani, who was born only a few years after the hall was opened, had been exposed to so much praise for the acoustics of the hall that now he simply accepted the idea that the acoustics of the hall were famous without question. It was possible that the acoustics of the hall weren't famous at all; that the phrase had been used in a publicity leaflet during the month the hall opened and somehow it had stuck, possibly because nobody could think of other interesting things to say about the place. Even today, everybody in this town believed that the acoustics of the hall were famous. People who'd only ever stood outside the hall mentioned the fact, when walking past with visitors, that the acoustics of the hall were famous. To Jani, the 'modern' concert hall, with its cleverly angled concrete surfaces, did seem to resonate with sound. But whenever he travelled to other cities, Jani never noticed anybody talking about the famous acoustics that could be found in the hall where he came from. In a way this made the famous acoustics even more significant. Their fame was a kind of secret which only a few cognoscenti had knowledge of. Jani turned his head away from the dancers on stage to check the upturned faces of his family; they all watched, open mouthed.

They clapped, they laughed and gasped and snivelled. Then, during the interval the crowd became its own spectacle: an army dressed in its finery. The air in the bars was thick with goodwill as charming words rebounded off the curved concrete and beach wood walls of the atrium. Everybody felt good. Jani's wife even smiled at him. Jani knew that she suspected he hadn't told her the full story but she seemed genuinely moved by the efforts he was making. At least her mother and their children seemed to have no idea that there could be anything wrong. They didn't know that Jani, having confessed to have needed some time alone, had grovelled on his knees in an effort to persuade his wife to come to the ballet. Jani's wife touched his arm.

'Thanks,' she said. 'They are really enjoying themselves.'

Their children and her mother were deep in conversation over tubs of ice cream.

Jani smiled nervously.

Then he excused himself, to visit the toilet. He made his way through the suits and dresses towards the cloakrooms, which were situated at the side of the atrium. Just as he reached the door, a cold hand grabbed his wrist and yanked at it. Jani deviated from the path to the men's toilets and was pulled into the cloakroom. Before he could react Jani found himself encased in a muffling mass of furs, woollens and mackintoshes. His head protruded over the sea of coats and scarves twitching like a cormorant's. He could still feel the cold hand on his wrist but whoever the hand belonged to remained concealed beneath the canopy of outer-garments. Jani tried to grab the wrist with his free hand. Another cold hand latched onto his free arm and then deftly clamped his wrists together behind his back with a pair of handcuffs.

'What's going on?' hissed Jani – staring across the coats. He was drawn further from the door, deeper into the coats. The cloakroom had a counter that was open to public inspection. If he turned his head Jani could see out into the atrium and the crowd of ballet fans. He could see his mother-in-law, his wife, his children, the ice cream.

'OK – who is this – what's going on? Is this some kind of joke?'

Like a swimmer who takes a breath before diving below the surface, Jani filled his lungs and stuffed his head into the river of coats. He tried to break free, rapidly, waving his clamped wrists in all directions, trying to unsettle his assailant. But it was impossible to see down there. He surfaced spitting dust and wool.

Then he felt the hands on his trousers – unbuttoning them, loosening them, then pulling them down, so that they restricted his feet.

'Get lost,' hissed Jani, who now could no longer take steps from side to side.

He felt the hands as they pushed his pants down.

'Fuck off,' he hissed. 'This is the fucking ballet.'

He realised who was down there. Jani glanced frantically into the atrium; nobody had noticed his head sticking up above the coats.

'I can't do this. I can't keep seeing you. I'm old. You're young. I'm married. You're single. You deserve better. You should have a proper boyfriend. I can see my wife and children... and my mother-in-law.'

Then, instead of cold hands he felt something wet and warm. He guessed it was her mouth. And strangely, he had also to guess (at first) that his assailant was sucking his cock. Somehow, the fact that he could not see his hands and that they were clamped together in an unnatural position and he'd lost control of his legs meant that he wasn't sure what any of his extremities were saying to him. Jani tried to hop away but he merely succeeded in losing his balance so that now he leaned, rather unsteadily, against a thick tweed overcoat. It was new and strong and it squashed against his nose. Then a disturbing possibility occurred to Jani. It was possible that the 'modern' concert had a perverted cloakroom attendant who made a habit of doing unmentionable things to fish that swam too far away from the shoal. He wriggled and writhed but he could not dislodge himself from the tightly packed coats. The more he tried to break free, the tighter the coats pressed in on him. The buzzer went to indicate that the performance was about to resume. Jani let out a whimper as he watched his wife scanning the atrium for him. He forced his head under the coats and hissed into the fabric.

'You lunatic, leave me alone!'

But the assailant didn't. The buzzer went again and the crowd began filing back towards their seats. Jani watched his wife, guiding the girls and her mother into the auditorium.

He returned to his seat late. He looked as if he had just run to Belgium and back. His hair stood on end and his clothes hung unevenly on his body. He shrugged at his wife, as if to say that he had been inadvertently dealing with some business. She paid no attention to him.

'I met a colleague from school in the toilets,' whispered Jani. 'He cornered me about next year's baccalaureate papers – boy he can go on.'

'Thank you for bringing us,' she whispered. 'It's just wonderful.'

Jani scanned the auditorium searching for the girl. Was she disguised as an usher? Standing on the stage in the chorus? Turning the pages for the kettle drum player? He knew she was there, watching him, enjoying the famous acoustics.

THURSDAY, OCTOBER 17TH

'Adenosine is a very important molecule. Right down there, at a sub-cellular level, it's adenosine who keeps life ticking along. It transfers energy from one place to another. I love adenosine. Now, if you think about the first thing – transferring energy, all of it, that's quite a responsibility. But here's another one. Love is the concept that doesn't exist in science, but is all over our nature. Isn't that strange? We love each other, but not the things that we're made of. I feel that this has to be the most attractive molecule,' Janja smiled at the confused looking undergraduates ranged in front of her. She waived her hand towards an image of coloured hydrogen, oxygen and nitrogen atoms, projected onto the screen behind her. 'Try not to think of molecules as being just bunches of atoms, try get into their personalities.'

Some of the students – there were about thirty five of them in all – nodded from their benches, they looked at the molecule and tried to 'get' it.

'There are billions of molecules,' continued Janja. 'Just like there are billions of people. But there are more molecules than people, or at least, that's the way we see it in this part of the universe. Our minds are made out of some of those molecules, including this one. The molecules of our bodies are put together in such a way as to have preferences. The molecules in our brains have predilections for preferences. If you can see the personality of adenosine triphosphate, which I have drawn for you here, the adenosine triphosphate in your own bodies will be pleased. At this very moment, it's probably redoubling its efforts to keep you all metabolising. Because it knows you're thinking about it. It's getting little chemical messages. 'Be good. They're looking at us.' Now, you will never forget the name of this molecule and what it does.'

Janja tapped her papers on the desk.

'Next week we'll have a little look at what adenosine triphosphate, ATP, does. That's really going to rock your world.'

SUNDAY, OCTOBER 20TH

A week had passed before Clara returned to the car boot sale. Once again she wandered through the ranks of stalls and their exhibits of domestic archaeology. She looked for the Volvo lady and, with some relief, didn't find her. She bought a Le Creuset cooking pot, burnished orange on the outside, clotted cream within, oval in shape, deep, with a cracked lid. Then, after delaying her exit for as long as seemed reasonable, Clara made her way towards her destination. Now she felt excited. Would the shoddy little stall, the last stall, the one where she had bought the coat not so long ago still be there? She had a feeling that it would.

Although Clara pretended to have accidently stumbled upon the stall for the second time, in fact, her entire journey around the airfield had been structured around her final visit. By the time she began pushing her way towards the way out, Clara was bursting with anticipation. When she saw the stall she felt elated because, for once, she had not been disappointed. This time, amongst the tooth brush chargers, the worn out Dutch paratrooper's boots and the lonely plastic toys, she found the boots – beautiful, black leather Italian boots. She saw the toys pointing out from under the rickety plastering table, she touched them gently, almost as if she was extending her fingers towards the black and shiny nose of an unknown and possibly snappy dog. Her fingers came to rest on the smooth tips of the boots and slowly she pulled them out from their den beneath the table. They were delicate but strong. The heels were like towers. She bought them for less than the price of her broken cooking pot with the broken lid.

At home that night Clara put on her coat and boots for the first time. The coat was a little big and the boots quite tight. Clara knew that the clothes were undisciplined, they had already had at least one life, but now they had to be made to fit their new owner and forget the old one. Clara gazed at her reflection in her mirror. She pouted. She hadn't pouted for years. Normally speaking she felt too dowdy to pout, but now these clothes reminded her that she did own a pout. She looked quizzically at herself. Sexy or stupid? It was hard for her to tell. The boots and the coat were fine but the face... the hair. She recognised those from the reflection in the windscreen on her bus. They lacked colour, contrast, definition. They were bored and boring. Standing there, in front of her mirror, in the coat and the boots, Clara could see that her eyes had lost their sparkle. But at the very moment she looked into them - her eyes, that is - they sparkled. It was as if her eyes and the boots and the coat were in it together, which was impossible. So she laughed. Clara remembered the girl on the bus. Her face was made up like a painting. Now she could see why. The coat and the boots would not wear anything else.

MONDAY, OCTOBER 21ST

The moon slipped away from another night and the sunlight swept across this small part of the surface of the earth, playing its usual trick, concealing its endless headlong dash with a pyrotechnic display which people called 'dawn'. Men, because they cannot see the whole, misinterpret this. It gives them the feeling of a beginning but dawn is just the topple point in a falling line of dominos, it is not the really the start of a new day, it is part of an everlasting tumble. So reasoned the Dormouse Master, as he watched the sun come up.

The Dormouse Master took every opportunity to observe sunrises. From his high vantage point in the hills he could make out features almost a hundred miles away. He could see enough land to watch the light of dawn chasing shadows down the sides of valleys. With this in mind, it was comparatively easy to imagine the sunrise a few hours earlier in Central Siberia, or before that in the Pacific or before that in Nevada or before that in the Bay of Biscay or before that here again, on his mountain. That was as far back as the Dormouse Master usually went, although once he spent three days dwelling on the search for the beginning of the day, trying to move further and further backwards in time. He failed because he lost count, just as a child forgets how many 'greats' to put in front of a distant antecedent. The Dormouse Master concluded that the sunrise, apparently unique and spectacular, an age-old symbol of the start of things, an activator of human time itself, was, at the very least, yesterday's. The sunrise did not belong to today at all. It came from the day before, and the day before that and the day before - it was an old dog chasing its tail. The real question, the only question, The Dormouse Master realised, was this: when was the first sunrise? When was the only sunrise?

In fact, the Dormouse Master reasoned, the whole idea of day and night was yet another convenient concoction, a mis-description, a means of hiding what was really going on. Whenever he was late for an appointment the Dormouse Master was fond of saying that time flows like a river without banks - like the water in a puddle without a hole to hold it. Sometimes it trickles like a tear across a face, other times it rushes like a stream of traffic on a motorway. Hours are not measurements of time, they are stories full of minutes, seconds and nanoseconds. A while back, it was with regard to this notion that the Dormouse Master had decided to conduct another of his experiments. For two months, the Dormouse Master abandoned clock time altogether, sleeping whenever he wanted and hunting at unconventional hours. He was eventually persuaded to return to a more conventional routine by a delegation of chefs from the city's top restaurants who had grown tired of receiving their deliveries of dormice at irregular intervals, usually in the middle of the night, when all their customers had gone home to bed

Today was different. It was the day of the Dormouse Master's hearing. The Dormouse Master was going to use the clock.

* * *

The centre of town glowed, grape gold in morning light. This particular bridge over the river, the one the children call 'Three Bridges' was built with the rhythms of human life in mind, disrupting them. The bridge, or bridges, because there are three spans, in parallel, not in sequence, conducts traffic as if the architect had decided to create a slow movement. Unlike the one with the dragons, this bridge only has room for two, not four, lanes of traffic. And there is a kink in the main road midstream which makes acceleration dangerous. Most interestingly of all, there are two separate promenades, wider than pavements but not broad enough for cars. The promenades and the road give drivers and pedestrians the impression that each is on the point of invading the other's space - it keeps them vigilant. It was built by such a clever architect.[1]

---

1. *The architect who built the three bridges built many of this town's best buildings.*

A woman, elderly, wearing a tweed suit, driving a small red car, made her way carefully across the bridge. She gripped her steering wheel with both hands, anxious not to be put off track by the sound of cobbles under her tires, the beauty of the white marble colonnades in the early morning sunlight and the sweet smelling autumnal air.

A man gazed down from his office window. He watched the little red car negotiate the delicate concoction of bridges joining the river-side cafes with the market square. Almost all of the pumpkins on the market stall, he noticed, had been hollowed out and etched with faces. He suspected that they wouldn't keep until the end of the month: anyone buying one now would have to get a replacement. From the car, his eyes flicked upwards, not to the sky but to the castle, almost rocking, like a grounded galleon on an outcrop of rock. The castle had spent the last century entertaining two kinds of visitors: tourists, chattering and snapping its walls - and prisoners, trying to imagine them away. It was the prisoners, he realised as he stroked his smooth chin, who would have paid the architecture of the castle serious attention and who, ultimately, must have grown to appreciate its builders' skill and hard work, because they would have been trying to work out how to get out.

Slabo, Minister for Culture, pushed his grey hair back across the top of his head and moved away from the window. He had slept in the office (there was a comfortable settee), he had showered in the office (he had an en suite bathroom), he had breakfasted at the office vending machine on crisps and old apple, he had put on fresh clothes (he kept a wardrobe at work) and he had shaved (he had a Philips three headed electric razor in the draw of his desk). The question was, could he get out? The answer was: of course he could. He was dapper again.

OK, so he shagged a few tarts. Half the government were trolling around the car parks near the ring road in search of experiences that might grant them temporary relief from the pressures of pretending to be other people. A week or so ago he was a broken man split into three parts: 'The Dog', 'The King' and 'The Intermediary'. He had discovered an elusive extra self, the one he named Not Number Four, and several others. Then he had rejected them all. Today Slabo was feeling better, a single rounded character. Kings were supposed to be dogs. Charles II of England had at least 19 children, Louis XIV had populated most of the French aristocracy with his own offspring, Leopold IX of Baden Baden, or perhaps it was somewhere else, or even someone else, was famous for one thing and one thing only – the length of his bratwurst. Good kings were good fucks. There was no problem. As for the writer, Slabo had already taken care of him. It was obvious that Not Number Four was the product of a sleep deprived mind on the edge of an existential precipice. Such things, Slabo knew, did not exist.

Slabo straightened his tie. No, his problem was that he was too fond of life, not that it was too much for him. He had not committed murder, some other fool had taken his rash words out of context. Well, if that nut case had to be found and got rid of – so be it. But no more pissing about in cars with Vala. The removal of the miscreant would be handled professionally.

It was a big city, but not that big. There were only three hired guns at work who could be trusted. Two of them were on long term contractual work abroad. The third, Zebedee, had never had it so good.

* * *

An hour later Slabo pulled up in his Black BMW outside the old barracks in the Black Forest district. He was alone, Vala was at her apartment. Slabo stepped out of his car and sucked in fresh air. He stared at the huge building in front of him: wooden sash windows splintering and buckling, glass smashed, roof raided for lead, walls bulging with dampness.

The seventeenth century barracks building used to house the Royal Regiment of Heavy Infantry, until they were moved to the countryside, before they were disbanded. In the beginning, the regiment was the best equipped and feared most fighting force in Europe and this barracks was the talk of professional military men from Buenos Aires to Moscow.

By the end of the eighteenth century things had changed. For one thing, the city had expanded and the musket ranges and parade grounds that used to surround the barracks had largely been sold off and filled with new housing developments. And things were never really the same after the Napoleonic era. Although he called himself an Emperor, the diminutive invader embodied two things many of his conquered subjects secretly admired – people power and the possibility of change. After he left, the merchants and artisans who had come to live near the barracks grew restless. They didn't feel their houses were quite French enough to reflect their developing social status. The old ghetto fell into disrepair as the nouveau riche established grander residences on the East side of town, where the tributaries of the river over which the Fat Dragons stand flow, where vines grow, where garden and town intermingle.[2]

During the 1830's the regiment, still quartered in its now dilapidated headquarters, was associated with slums, blunderbusses and syphilis. It was during this period that this quarter was given its name: the Black Forest. Hardly a week went by without someone being killed in a duel in its dark and dangerous hinterland. The region, which covered no more than a square kilometre, became the haunt of drunks, prostitutes and, most famously of all, poets. It was here that Casper Kridpan, the great national icon of the nineteenth century literature wrote his ground breaking-work 'Love'. It was published in 1848 and has never been out of print.[3] Kridpan, a lawyer from the East Side, fell in love with a sixteen year old prostitute from

---

2. *Where, incidentally, the boys and their new friend Sabel met their attacker the previous evening.*
3. *Aside from the post-war period.*

The Black Forest. He was forty seven. One night, famously, he got into a fight with a soldier from the Royal Heavies who was rumoured to be the girl's father. There was a duel. Kridpan came off worse. Just like Pushkin himself, he died painfully, over a period of days. It was Kridpan's death, and his desire to write poems about it, that sealed his literary reputation. 'I Am Dying' remains a set text in all of this city's junior schools.

Eventually it was realised that the chief reason why the Black Forest district had such a bad reputation was because the soldiers from the barracks had been supporting an economy based on vice for hundreds of years. Drink, drugs, sex and violence – all were enjoyed by the soldiers and they were paid for by the tax payers, most of whom lived as far away from the barracks as possible - in the bucolic part. It was decided that the only way to improve things was to close the barracks. The plan worked with devastating results. The theatres and cafes, which were an important part of Black Forest, life also closed. Not only that, the academic institutions which were originally endowed by the prostitutes of the Black Forest, anxious to improve the lot of their children, moved away.

The Black Forest became an even darker place, infested with hopelessness. Its decaying buildings, which many members of the intelligentsia had come to realise were Romantic and worthy of preservation, collapsed.

Slabo shivered in the porch of the old barracks, dwarfed by the size of the strange, cuboid eight legged portico which had been attached to the front of the building during the nineteen thirties. At that time the barracks was used as a sanatorium; during the Second World War it became a munitions depot; after that, a hospital.

The odour seeping from the building entered and became Slabo. It reminded him of marzipan and old leaves, although, perhaps, intermingled with the spores and rot, there remained in the air just the faintest hint of disinfectant, or gin.

'It's been like this for twenty years,' a silky voice slid into the vestibule.

Slabo jumped, he turned on his heels, unable, immediately, to identify the source of the words.

A thin white face appeared in the gap between the two tall rusting doors. Slabo was surprised, he was expecting the grizzled face of a life-time mercenary, but this man's skin was soft and milky, his moustache was indistinct, his eyes dark and sad. With some difficulty the man prized the heavy metal doors apart. They ground the concrete threshold, chipping off flakes.

'Architecturally, it's a trickster,' he said, ushering Slabo in. 'The original barracks is virtually untouched inside, from the outside it looks like a piece of totalitarian cinema kitsch'. Slabo thought he sounded like a wealthy aristocrat welcoming tourists into his own private mansion.

'Really,' said Slabo, who was not in the slightest bit interested in the history of the building or the surrounding area. It was all one big shithole as far as he was concerned.

As he led Slabo into the vast entrance hall, the man continued to speak as if he owned the place, as if he was personally responsible for its upkeep.

'The grand staircase has gone, and the fireplaces, and most of the floors, but the plaster mouldings are still on the ceilings and the frescos are comparatively fresh. There's a beautiful one of the battle of Thermopile in the gymnasium,' he said, as they picked his way over the cakey floorboards.

'Really,' said Slabo, again.

They reached another door. It was made of oak. The man leant on it and it creaked open, revealing a library full of rotting books, long tables and broken angle poise lamps. Dust hung in the air, making it seem watery, difficult to wade through.

'They're all medical books,' said the man, noticing Slabo gawp at the height of the bookcases, the precarious looking ladders, the collapsing walkways and the robotic iron filing cabinets. 'You remember the hospital?'

Slabo nodded as he stepped slowly into the room. This place was famous, the president had died in it.

The man held his hand out:

'I'm Zebedee, I believe you have something for me, Slabo.'

Slabo looked at Zebedee. He was weedy, like a liquorice root, wearing black trousers, black shoes and a black polo neck sweater. His hair was black. Slabo produced an envelope from his pocket and handed it over. Zebedee took it and placed it on a table.

'I'd say it feels about right,' he said.

'What?' asked Slabo.

'The package,' said Zebedee.

'Do people still live in here?' asked Slabo, sniffing the ratty, catty air.

'A few,' replied Zebedee. 'Dying people. They hide in the rafters. They're probably watching us now. It's only because they know that I'm armed that they stay in the shadows. Sometimes they run out, begging for me to shoot them. These are forgotten people, terminally ill, homeless, hopeless.'

Slabo peered into the shadows, he listened. But he could see nothing and he heard only the purring of pigeons high up in the shelves.

'Maybe I saw a shape in that corner,' said Slabo.

'Don't lie,' said Zebedee. 'You can't see anything in here. It's too dark and you're too certain of yourself. To you this is merely an empty building that should have been pulled down years ago. You have no idea that now it is a village full of desperate human beings who scream in terror during the nights, when they are forced to contemplate the utter futility of their lives, when they are driven to contrast the hope with which they started out and the despair that they have exchanged it for. You cannot see that you are the same as them, that all you have done is delay the moment of realisation by pretending to be an optimist. Who do you want me to kill?'

'A man called Garibaldi,' said Slabo. 'He worked in my department.'

'A reasonable request,' said Zebedee, stroking his chin. 'Garibaldi?' he asked.

'Drago Garibaldi, he's an administrator,' said Slabo.

'Is this merely a bureaucratic matter or has he transgressed in some wider context?' asked Zebedee.

'It was a big mistake. He misunderstood. I think he thought I asked him to kill a girl. He killed her. If the police find him he will confess, he'll tell them I instructed him, but I didn't. I just said, in passing, that I wished someone would get rid of her. You have to be so careful what you say if you are in my position. She was a beautiful woman.'

'Did you love her?' asked Zebedee.

'Why do you ask?' asked Slabo.

'I need to understand,' said Zebedee.

'She was a prostitute,' said Slabo.

'Is that supposed to change things?' asked Zebedee.

'No,' said Slabo, 'I suppose not. I have to go... And don't be so ridiculous.'

Slabo walked slowly towards the door. Zebedee moved behind a table. He pushed his finger into a gap at the top of the envelope and began to tear it open.

'Thank you,' said Zebedee. 'If you have any messages for me, leave them on the notice-board on the wall in here. You won't be seeing me again.'

Zebedee waived his hand at a pin board covered in fading green baize just next to the door.

'When I have news for you, you will know. Bonaparte will be dead within a week.'

Slabo turned.

'Garibaldi.'

Zebedee glanced up from the money, which he was counting.

'A new name, Slabo. Never accurately name the one you are about to kill. It causes the formation of a vapour trail.'

Slabo hurried back through the staircase-less lobby, through the great door into the strange porch, with its tentacular supports, out into the air and finally into his car. He sped off, eastwards, as fast as he could.

*   *   *

It was an hour before midday. Sunshine stung the surfaces of the clean glasses and mirrors in the odd little bar. Jani lurched in, shielding his eyes from the glare. He ordered a coffee and a glass of brandy.

He sipped the frothy top off his coffee and poured the brandy into it, glancing up at the Halloween decorations that had been pinned to the ceiling: cobwebs and spiders. At least, he assumed they were decorations. His brow furrowed as he tried to focus on them. Surely they were too big to be real.

'You want to watch that,' said a familiar voice.

It was Priest.

'Brandy for lunch is the precursor of lager for breakfast.'

'Oh God,' said Jani.

'Come and join us at a table, tell us your latest problem,' said Smoke beckoning cheerily.

'Isn't it obvious?' asked Priest, taking a chair.

They sat at small, circular marble-topped table where four beer mats had been carefully placed, so as to resemble compass points.

'It wasn't my fault,' moaned Jani.

'He's at it again,' said Priest.

Jani looked resentfully at Priest and Smoke, as the third, the fat one tapped away at the quiz machine. Jani had noticed that he had some kind of official relationship with the barman. Sometimes he collected glasses and occasionally he would disappear underground to do something to a barrel.

'There's no need to tell us what happened,' said Smoke, finishing his drink.

'I wasn't going to,' said Jani.

'We know,' said Priest, with a smile.

The three of them sat in silence, all apparently contemplating Jani's predicament and his weaknesses. Priest didn't speak, he nodded his head and held Jani's gaze with his own fluffy brown eyes as if to say:

'We all do bad things. Perhaps the more active amongst us have more opportunity to make mischief. Maybe those who stay indoors or cultivate their gardens, cause less damage by doing less. But every one of us has something to be ashamed about.'

Jani coughed. He couldn't look at Priest any more. He didn't know what he was supposed to be thinking. He was just nodding.

'You shouldn't harm other people, especially those you say you love,' said Jani.

'But a life with no pain is no life at all,' said Priest, raising his glass. 'Damage and destruction are the parents of creation.'

A bead of condensation grew on the side of an upturned glass somewhere up behind the bar. It burst and jinked downwards. It flowed over a glass shelf, following the trail of long gone droplets and then it fell, glimmering like a star before disappearing into the shadows down behind the counter. Priest gazed into the distance, Smoke stared into his empty glass, Jani fidgeted with his thoughts. Should he publish a letter in the local newspaper admitting his shame, confessing in public, apologising? That, at least, would be honest. He would lose the dreadful feeling growing inside him, that people, even complete strangers, needed to know the level of his treachery. Hiding the events at the ballet, and others, meant Jani felt like a fraudster, as if he was pretending to be something he was not. But would public humiliation really achieve anything? Would it make his children happy? What would his wife say?

'There must be a way of retrieving the situation,' said Jani.

'You mean, to redeem yourself?' asked Priest.

'I've been staring at this glass for ten minutes,' announced Smoke. 'It's empty, are neither of you going to buy me a drink?'

'Better get him one,' said Priest to Jani.

Jani stepped up to the bar. He ordered four glasses of beer. Perhaps, buying the drinks made him feel better because that's when his idea came. He would make a list. He would write down all things that had gone wrong, with dates and locations, precisely. He would define what moral codes they transgressed and decide how each one could be redeemed, either by apologising, or by helping the people involved or even by tying to make amends in other ways. He returned to the table and began to elaborate his new plan.

* * *

'The second most important feature of a planned transport policy (apart from the advantages already outlined; namely: efficient movement of goods and people from place to place) is environmental.'

Niko looked out of his bedroom window. The morning was caustically bright. Not the right weather for rewriting essays. He had a choice, he could consider environmental issues or he could become environmental himself.

He left his desk and went to see how the old man was doing.

*   *   *

The Dormouse Master thumped the desk with his fist. He snorted disapproval. Opposite him sat a small man in his early forties wearing a dark blue suit, it was a little too large for him and its buttons were silver. He was calm and serene. He watched the Dormouse Master with an amused, quizzical expression.

'It is normal, in these circumstances, for applicants to seek professional representation,' said Mr Frayling, of the Office of Intellectual Property.

'I don't need a brief,' shouted the Dormouse Master. 'I know who I am, everybody knows who I am, even you admit that you know who I am. So why is it forbidden that I should be able to protect my name by registering it as a trade mark?'

Mr Frayling placed his hands carefully on the mighty table in front of him. He sucked in some air. The vast spaces spreading out on either side of him were like the Hungarian plains; the hands were cathedrals, or capital cities, maybe Buda and Pest. He drummed his fingers, as if tapping up the spirits of long gone decision makers, soaking up their knowledge, their power. Now he filled his suit.

'Look, Mr... Master.'

'Dormouse Master,' growled the Dormouse Master.

'Dormouse Master, we have been over this before, several times.

The issue is not whether or not you are recognised by your name. What is at stake here is whether your name satisfies certain legal requirements necessary to permit registration under the terms of the 1956 Act. Unfortunately, according to the legal tests, the term 'Dormouse Master' just isn't distinctive.'

'But it is, everybody knows who I am.'

'No they don't, you cannot possibly know everyone.'

'I cannot be responsible for people I've never met.'

'If I may be permitted to introduce you to some precedents. These are cases in which similar issues have been explored and decided: whilst I am not bound by them, I often use them to assist in my deliberations. They are the sort of thing that, if you had a legal representative, that representative might make use of.'

The Dormouse Master nodded.

'Don't just pick ones from your side.'

'I wasn't going to,' said Mr Frayling. 'I don't want to be unfair to you. The Backhouse case, for example, makes it clear that when a name is composed of two dictionary words – in this case 'back' and 'house' - it is possible for the whole, the totality, to be regarded as what is a called 'a coalescence not a partial name'. Thus, names like 'Greenhat', 'Fishford' and 'Applecake' may, under certain circumstances, be registered.'

The Dormouse Master nodded, unconvinced, he'd never met anyone called Greenhat, Fishford or Applecake.

'However,' continued Frayling, 'the 'Pickend' case, quite a landmark decision, also establishes that if a consumer would, in all likelihood, overlook the ordinary signification of the neologism formed by a coalescence, then the correct decision may still be to reject the mark on the basis of an absence of what was described in the decision as a 'strikingly provocative conceptual capacity'. Pickend, famously, did not have sufficient 'duality of significance', nor was its concept, the end of a pick, sufficiently inventive to distance the word from the fact that, in any directory of telephone numbers, either online or in paper form, there are usually as many as five Pickends to be found, proving that, in the end, Pickend is, first and foremost, a surname. Do you see what I mean?'

The Dormouse Master nodded.

'Dormouse Master', I would argue, is almost on all fours with Pickend, although the term 'Master', adds a third, and perhaps even more untenable aspect to the mark. 'Master' practice is referred to in all our guidelines and it was established way back, in 1897, that 'Master' when allied to a descriptive suffix or prefix actually detracts from the distinctive potential of a mark by imparting a laudatory signification which, as far as 360 degree perception of a trade mark is concerned, renders any word within a country mile of the term 'master' dead in the water. It is not a fancy phrase – it is an ordinary one, you just think it is, because you rather fancy yourself.'

Mr Frayling smiled.

'How many other people called Dormouse Master do you know?' growled the Dormouse Master.

'How many people called 'Man Who Works At The Petrol Station' do you know? retorted the Dispute Resolution Officer.

The Dormouse Master, who had been standing, slumped down on his chair. He stared up at the high ceiling, with its strip lights, incongruously jammed over an ornate ceiling rose. He turned and considered the grand arched window behind Frayling, the wooden floor, the fireplace, now blocked with a bust of a famous judge, the green painted walls, the fat old radiators and the small desk where the typist sat, fingers flying over her keys as she recorded the conversation for publication.

The typist was nearing retirement age. When she left she would not be replaced, the need for recording minutes in this way having been overtaken by technology. But until the day came for her to go, the woman, in her tweed suit, with her neat grey hair tied back into a bun, would keep the job, which according to the regulations, she was entitled to. The terms and conditions of state employees did not create millionaires, but there were no beggars on the books either.

Although the lady's face was heavily powdered, colourless and somewhat tired-looking, her fingers, which had spent forty years being exercised like Olympic gymnasts, were strong, supple and vivacious. She never missed a letter. They caught every syllable and recorded it for publication in the Official Book of Trade Marks Applications and Disputes, commonly referred by specialists as 'The Book'. It was an objective record of cases and their facts. There was no room for personal expression in The Book. Lists of marks, disputes and decisions and administrative changes were presented without embellishment. Forty years ago the typist adhered rigorously to this house style, or lack of it, but she learned, quite early on, that a trait that could be attributed only to her may be useful. When cases came up for review, even if she had forgotten whether or not she was the one who typed the decision, she would know because she secretly introduced her own unique mark into the text. Nobody had noticed, but her decisions always contained, somewhere in the text, an exclamation mark. It was her trade mark.

'You bastard,' growled the Dormouse Master, leafing through his muddy pile of letters.

'You bastard,' she wrote. Her left little finger hovered over the exclamation mark. After the tiniest hesitation she hit it and a smile rippled over her lips.

Nobody else worked liked this. The new clerks transcribed from digital recordings. But Alice had developed such speed and dexterity that she could transcribe a decision, without errors, during the proceedings.

That was not the only extraordinary thing about Alice. Over the years she had developed such familiarity with the enclave of trade marks law, where there is little room for combatants to indulge in discursive pyrotechnics, that all of the arguments had become familiar. She could summarise proceedings without paying attention; she recognised the gambits and precedents as a chess grand master spots openings. Her fingers seemed able to negotiate the long paragraphs, the claims and counterclaims, the references to the administrative manual without going to the trouble of deep thought (except where exclamation marks were concerned). So whilst Alice's hands were fully occupied on the keyboard, capturing the essentially, as she saw them, mechanical stories of the disputes, her mind was racing into other realms.

Mr Frayling, who sometimes wore suits with gold buttons, had given up asking Alice what she thought of his decisions. Alice could never remember what he had decided. She would always say the same thing:

'You were very fair Mr Frayling.'

In fact, as she sat and pounded out Mr Frayling's decisions, other entirely fictional conversations and scenarios condensed in Alice's mind. There would be passionate encounters in endless forests, there would be princes and kings. Castles, soothsayers, mountains, armies and falcons flapped and pranced around her head, as her finger dance gave everyone the impression that she was fully occupied with the law. Alice sold the fictional content of her hearings with Mr Frayling to a local publisher of romantic fiction. She'd created a novel writing persona for herself, Clara Fray. She was quite successful.

'I now have to ask you this question,' said Mr Frayling, fiddling with one of his buttons.

'But I haven't finished,' said the Dormouse Master.

'I am formally cautioning you,' said Frayling. 'We can't sit here all day contradicting one another.'

The Dormouse Master thought for a moment.

'Yes we can,' he said.

Mr Frayling smiled patiently.

'No,' he said. 'We can't.'

'Well I'm not going to agree with you, so I don't see what the alternative is,' said the Dormouse Master.

'I am informing you that this hearing has now, in my opinion, dealt with all of the significant relevant facts and that unless you have any new information, hitherto unseen by the court, I am empowered to bring proceedings to a close. I believe all reasonable avenues have now been explored and ask you, Mr Dormouse Master, to sign this statement accepting the rejection of your application to register the name 'Dormouse Master' as a Badge Of Origin.'

'My name is distinctive.'

'Are you formally refusing to sign the acceptance of rejection form?' asked Mr Frayling patiently.

Alice's fingers rattled the keys.

'Yes.'

'Could I ask you to sign this one instead?' asked Mr Frayling, pushing a yellow form towards the Dormouse Master's side of the table.

'What is it?' he asked warily, his hand touching the paper like a bear handling a poisoned salmon.

'It's a rejection of rejection form. It states that you do not accept my argument and gives you the right to lodge an appeal at the Grand Court within fifty seven days,' said Mr Frayling helpfully. 'You're quite at liberty to do this. It just means that the transcript of this Hearing will be drafted into an official decision which the Grand Court will use as a basis for its decision. We can resume this discussion there. To be honest with you, I quite enjoy writing decisions and I always relish the opportunity to go to court, especially where there is an interesting point of law to debate.'

'Is this interesting?' asked the Dormouse Master.

'Fascinating,' said Mr Frayling.

'Have you ever lost?' asked the Dormouse Master.

Mr Frayling shook his head with a smile.

'Its nine nil to me at the moment.'

The Dormouse Master grunted and signed the paper. Mr Frayling stood up and shook the Dormouse Master by the hand. The Dormouse Master shuffled out, carrying with him a plastic bag containing his correspondence, summaries of his arguments and some leaflets on crime prevention he had been given when he arrived at the court, and his pencils.

The door swung shut behind the Dormouse Master and Mr Frayling closed his pink file.

'Shame,' he said to Alice. 'He was a nice bloke.'

Alice recorded these words at the end of her transcript. She looked at Mr Frayling, erasing an image of two lovers meeting in a secret garden, with a lake and a clam-shell covered bridge, on a hillside, overlooking Trieste, as the sun set on the Adriatic, with the sound of cicadas crackling in the air and the heat of hot breath on the neck.

'Pardon Mr Frayling', she said.

'Nothing,' said Mr Frayling, shall we get ourselves some coffee before the next case?'

Alice nodded. As they walked to the canteen deep in the heart of the building, Alice asked if she could be excused for ten minutes. She had arrived later than usual and hadn't been able to park in the mezzanine, her little red car was on a meter.

Mr Frayling touched a button.

'How do you think it went?' he asked.

'You were very fair,' came the reply.

TUESDAY, OCTOBER 22ND

Clara flung the bus around another corner. Her collar was upright, rubbing into her ears, and her feet kept falling off the pedals. She glanced into her rear view mirror, her red lips snarled as she chastised all the drivers around. She felt fantastic, she looked down at the thigh length boots, her feet looked so sexy in their footwell. As soon an opportunity presented itself she stepped on the gas and moved into the fast lane.

'Fuck,' she whispered, 'my feet are so horny.'

She ran her tongue around her upper lip as she ploughed through the traffic, her coat and boots completely obliterating any sign of the navy-blue trousers and bright green sweater that belonged to the bus company.

WEDNESDAY, OCTOBER 23RD

Behind her, next to her office pin board was a big glossy picture of adenosine triphosphate. It came from a pull out in Scientific American. The atoms were coloured in orange, red, blue, and grey. They looked like an inter-stellar caterpillar, chewing its way through the wall. Janja had been working on this molecule for most her adult life. But like many people who know something or someone well, she felt that additions to the data already accumulated usually pointed towards more complexity and greater potential for misunderstanding rather than the opposite. Her search for and discovery of knowledge had produced an unexpected result – insecurity.

Indeed, although Janja knew more now about ATP than she had, say, ten years ago, she wasn't certain that she could say the same about herself. How could it be that an expert, a person known throughout the world as a one of the most knowledgeable human beings as far as this little molecule was concerned, should find herself in the grip of such powerful uncertainty? These days, whenever she spoke about adenosine triphosphate she explained that she could no longer decide whether she chose it or it found her. In her mind the character of ATP had become so strong that it was almost real, like a person.

Janja thought about Peter. He was probably at work with his new partner. Perhaps they were planning a holiday.

Janja made a note on a pad of paper. She was fond of notes. When it came to Peter, she found that the act of writing something down temporarily exorcised the disturbing feeling that the world made no sense and that she was falling, like a childhood favourite of hers, down a surprisingly big rabbit hole. Her office was full of notes and scribbles, all bearing aphorisms about what a shit Peter was, none successfully defining why. When her search for the formula for Peter was at its worst she'd scribble notes about him wherever she went. She'd store them in her pockets, the glove compartment of her car, her brief-case would fill up with them. She would find herself at the paper shop, scrabbling with her hands through dozens of aphorisms written on the back of bus tickets, supermarket receipts and demands for lost library books. If Janja found money for her newspaper she often didn't spend it because she'd written important messages on the notes. There was a week when Janja did little more than write haikus about her ex-partner on any available surface. At the end of the week, after failing to attend lectures or find the perfect phase, she was told that things had to change.

So Janja began to collect the week's 'work' up in blue plastic bags. Every Friday she put it out with the other laboratory waste. For a time her output remained high but perhaps the realisation that her attempts to define, in one line, the problem with her relationship, were going to end up in the bin at the end of the week, reduced her enthusiasm for the task. The evidence suggested that she would never get it right. That didn't mean she couldn't get it right. But since, in all honesty, she didn't really know what IT was, she concluded that there wasn't really any hope of meaningful success. So the papers went out every Friday and, gradually, she wrote less. These days she was averaging about four aphorisms about Peter a day.

Janja made a note:

'It's all yin and yang'

What she meant was that part of the difficulty of understanding what had happened with Peter was that for every minus there was a plus. It was like mitosis. Janja didn't write that down, she'd already explored almost every possible sub-cellular means of understanding her relationship with Peter.

She still remembered her times with him. The memories seemed unnaturally clear, sharper than anything real.

'It's not like yin and yang,' said Janja, with a practised smile, scrunching the yellow note up and flicking it at a grey metal dustbin, 'he steals all the stories.' Miraculously the little ball of paper sailed through the air and looped into the bin with a satisfying ping. Janja smiled. 'It's like yin and hydrochloric acid.'

Janja laughed. Things were getting better. She put that down to Gregor's intervention.

He was not in the least bit scientific or successful. He never did anything. He just grumbled. He revelled in obscurity. He regarded missing the point as somehow getting the point and he had the pleasing effect of making Peter, her former partner, look rather pompous. Gregor released Janja from regret, blame, loathing and longing. Janja's fictitious, ugly, fat, grumpy detective made Peter, her handsome, brilliant and real ex-partner look predictable and foolish.

The discovery that Peter might be unattractive was as important to Janja as the moons of Jupiter were to Galileo, but less so to everyone else.

THURSDAY, OCTOBER 24TH

She raised both hands to her head and placed the tips of her fingers on her temples. Her burgundy nails looked like droplets of blood on her pale, powdered skin. The truth was, she thought sadly, there was actually very little for her to consider. With a sigh she lifted her gaze and began making little circular motions to relieve the tension.

'What's his name again?' she asked.

'Zebedee,' said Slabo, from behind his desk. He seemed uneasy: 'You told me to sort it out – so I have.'

Vala took her head out of her hands and looked at the man opposing her.

'I resign,' she said firmly and stood up.

'Sit the fuck down,' said Slabo.

'Shut the fuck up,' she snapped and turned towards the door.

Slabo darted from behind his desk and rushed to the door.

'Oh no you don't,' he said. 'You can't walk out on me now.'

'I can and I will,' hissed Vala 'And if you don't let me out of this office now I'm going to turn this whole story over to the press.'

'Don't try to blackmail me.'

'I'm your adviser, Minister. I give advice. With my advice you have built a successful career. Without it you have caused one murder and ordered another. When you are discovered I want to be as far away from you as possible. You are the political equivalent of a suicide bomber.'

'Get back in your chair you fat cow,' hissed Slabo. He advanced on Vala shoving her back down into her chair.

Vala toppled but caught herself on the arms. She twisted and threw herself at Slabo knocking him off balance. He collapsed backwards towards the door, dropping sideways, cracking the back of his head on a filing cabinet. As he sank to the floor, shocked by the impact, Vala punched him in the face. A right then a left. Slabo shielded himself from the blows, thin strands of his grey hair toppling into his eyes.

'This is physical abuse,' screamed Vala, raining punches on the minister. 'I resign, you're fucked, one word from me and you're fucked, you let me go... now.'

The irony of the situation did not escape Slabo. Even in these reduced circumstances (he was the one receiving the blows) he was being asked to be less abusive. As a diamond encrusted zirconium ring punctured his right eyebrow, it occurred to him that this situation neatly summed his view of the nature of politics – it was a thankless task. He knew one thing for certain. He could not let Vala go, even if she beat him unconscious. With her on the loose his story would be out and he would find himself out in the cold for a very long time. He summoned all his political will, clenched his fist and landed a right hook on Vala's chin which sent her reeling across the room and onto the floor. Before she could recover, Slabo had scrambled to his feet. Slabo was able to wind her with a kick to the midriff. She wheezed uncomfortably and spat blood onto the carpet. Slabo leant on his desk, panting, mopping blood from his face with forearm.

'You fucking bitch.'

'I'll fucking kill you for this,' Vala crawled to the edge of the desk she pulled herself upright.

'Get back to your fucking chair and advise me, you fat cow.'

Vala, detecting that she had lost the upper hand and, noting the fact that Slabo was now armed with a titanium Siamese cat given to him by a delegation from the Federation of Chinese Metallurgists, sat in her chair. Slabo returned to his seat. Blood dripping down the side of his face onto his shirt. He sat down and leaned forwards.

'Zebedee will kill the miscreant, the case will be closed, we will be in the clear.'

'Didn't I tell you not to involve others. This Zebedee can blackmail you for ever now. You are a slave to him – don't you see – he is the minister now,' whispered Vala.

Slabo thought for a moment.

'We'll fix him later.'

'Blood will have blood.'

With a scream, Slabo threw the cat at Vala, it struck her on the shoulder. She winced with pain.

'That's not fucking advice. I want fucking advice.'

They sat opposite one another, breathing in short gasps. Neither Vala nor Slabo spoke for some time.

*   *   *

'And so, in conclusion, it can be seen that the physical effects of introducing new crop varieties to relatively underdeveloped economies can be harmful. It should also be remembered that it is within recent years that major irrigation projects have been shown to have limited usage in that they too can result in unforeseen damage. All this must be counterpointed with the arguments that progress is both inevitable and necessary. If it would not how would my previous arguments concerning integrated transport systems come to fruition? In conclusion, a balance must be struck between a scientific solution and the less quantifiable needs of everyday people.'

With a flourish, Niko banged his pen down on the desk. He picked up the mobile and called Laura. After some time she answered.

'Niko? Oh hi,' she said. She sounded ill, thought Niko.

'You sound ill babe. Hey, I've finished my essay, why don't you come over. Granddad's asleep, I've got loads of new soup.'

'No, I can't,' came the thin voice. 'Sorry'.

'You sound terrible,' said Niko. 'Shall I come over there, how are you feeling?'

'No I'm not ill.'

'You must be.'

'I'm not.'

'Well come over here then. We can do stuff with the soup. And you get to copy my essay. And I can tell you what happened. Exactly.'

Niko told Laura the story of Sabel, the man at the bridge, the brave rescue, the debacle with the cops, the fall-out with his family. It was days since he'd seen Laura. She seemed to have lost her old enthusiasm. She was quiet, almost reserved. If Niko had been talking to anyone else he'd have said that they were evasive.

A change had occurred. There was no use pretending.

'Babe, you're ill,' said Niko, 'I'll see you tomorrow. I love you.'

'Bye.'

Niko put the phone down. His eyes drifted to a plastic container in which half a portion of pumpkin soup lay defrosting.

FRIDAY, OCTOBER 25TH

The walk from the university to her flat took approximately twenty minutes. After fifteen minutes she arrived at the little shop. She stepped in.

Janja took her newspaper and exchanged the usual pleasantries with Karen. The exchange reassured Janja, it reassured Karen. For days Karen had been pestered by a succession of men and women trying to sell her security devices. It was good to see Janja from the university, always polite, preoccupied and dependable, a customer who visited at exactly the same time on her way to and from work.

Although Karen was right about the fact that Janja was almost always preoccupied. She was wrong about the subject of her deliberations. Janja wasn't thinking about fundamental laws, nor her students, nor her own adenosine trisulphide. She was thinking about a man who had disappeared. He was a fictional man, who didn't believe there was a story worth investigating in this town. He was a man who didn't exist, who couldn't see the point in existing. When Janja saw Karen she was grateful for the appearance of someone she knew to be real. Karen was reassured to see that Janja was still looking after the serious, difficult questions. They caught one another's eyes and were both surprised with the affection and intimacy in their glances. It was a moment of pure misunderstanding and also complete connection. In an instant each believed they understood one another – they became close.

SUNDAY, OCTOBER 27TH

In the woods outside town, at least two people were at work. The Dormouse Master, having laid his traps, started to fell trees. As he worked, he muttered to himself. He was right. He knew it. Human invention is protectable, natural phenomena are not. He was not claiming the ownership of dormice, he was not trying to patent their genome, he was simply anxious that the invented name by which hundreds of his customers knew him should not fall into the hands of a multinational conglomerate. Now (the pine trees were young here, their roots had not penetrated very deep into the soil) he uprooted trees with his bare hands. He carried them to the edges of the clearing. He worked in the dark, the moonlight shining silver on his sweating skin.

A shot rang out in the night.

The Dormouse Master froze, still as a deer. He listened. He guessed it was poachers. But it was ridiculous of them to come out shooting in the night.

*   *   *

Zebedee, dressed in black, with a black balaclava, a black rucksack on his back, black underpants, black socks, black trousers, black shoes and black gloves stood still, like a panther. He held his rifle to his shoulder, closed one eye, peered down the night sight, located the target and squeezed the trigger. This time there was no loud rapport echoing around the valley sides, the silencer had been fitted and it was working. Zebedee marched off towards the target; the bullet had blown an eight centimetre diameter hole seventeen centimetres deep in the trunk of a large chestnut tree. A human recipient of such a blow would be reduced to something quite amorphous even with an indirect hit. Pleased with the results, Zebedee began his descent through the forest. He was ready for the hunt.

*   *   *

Jani finally emerged from the bar and staggered onto an empty pavement. It was late again, all but a few were asleep. He lost impetus outside the big glass window of Nicolo's seafood restaurant. He peered in, it was a habit of his. He liked looking at the lobsters, their claws taped with elastic bands, perching on rocks in their tank. He wouldn't move on until he'd selected a succulent one.

Something caught Jani's eye. He squinted past the lobsters, into the dark recesses of the room. There, right at the back, a couple sat either side of a platter of fruits de la mer. A voluptuous woman in her late thirties, was peeling a langoustine with her fingernails, her long brown hair, held back from the sticky operation with an Alice band. He, older, with stringy grey hair, dissected a crab's claw with a pick. Both wore dark glasses, which cannot have helped them in their work, because the room they were in was uninvitingly gloomy, the predominant light source being the purple tubes in the lobster's tank. Jani pressed his face up against the glass, the lobsters rubbed their antennae along their pane, The woman had a swollen lip and bruised arm. The man appeared to have a bandage across his forehead. They drank swiftly from large wine glasses.

A voice disturbed him.

'Move away from the light and close your eyes.'

Jani obeyed.

'Take out your wallet,' continued the voice.

'Can I open my eyes?' asked Jani.

'If you want to die.'

Jani kept his eyes shut and found his wallet. He handed it to the man (it was a man's voice). The man took the cash from the wallet and handed it back.

'Keep your eyes closed for a minute and you'll be safe.'

Jani heard the man turn on his heels and run. As soon as the sound of footsteps hit the grass on the river bank, they became less easy to distinguish and they vanished. For good measure Jani stood still, with his eyes shut, for another minute. He opened his eyes. Three lobsters looked on critically.

Jani flipped his wallet open. All of his cards were there. The robber had only taken a few notes. Jani was on the point of bursting into the restaurant and asking for assistance from the two strange diners when he realised there was very little point. The police would come. He'd end up having to stay up even later, and in point of fact, he didn't have very much to complain about. If anything, he was rather grateful with the criminal for being so reasonable.

Jani hurried away. When he reached the bridge, the one with the dragons guarding it, he began to trot down the middle of the road. There was no traffic around and he felt safer as far away from the shadowy dark sides as possible.

But after Jani had crossed the bridge a car appeared, forcing him to run from the traffic lanes back onto the pavement. As he jogged around a lamp post something hit him. It sent him flying. He crashed down onto the pavement.

'You're very late.' This time it was a woman. Her voice sounded husky and deep, as if the true tone had been disguised. 'Close your eyes and stand up – before I kill you.'

She grabbed Jani. He tried to wriggle free. He stopped when he felt a cold point pressing painfully into the side of his neck.

'OK, OK,' he whispered, clamping his eyes shut and rising to slowly to his feet.

'Why are you jogging down the middle of the road in the middle of the night?' said the woman.

'I was scared,' said Jani. 'I was trying to stay in the light.'

'You nearly got yourself run over.'

'It was an oversight,' said Jani.

'Walk this way,' said the woman.

She pushed Jani back towards the bridge and the fat green dragons. They walked back across the bridge.

The woman told Jani to stop. He could hear her opening a door. Should he run and risk being stabbed, or simply step, like a meek animal, over the threshold and into the building without even opening his eyes? The assailant had been a gentleman. This one didn't feel so good.

'Can I open my eyes?' asked Jani.

He heard the woman push the door. It sounded heavy. The hinges creaked and the door scraped the threshold. Jani felt the steel in his neck again.

'No.'

She pushed him in.

Jani took a decision. He opened his eyes, as he tumbled into the lobby of an old apartment block. He glimpsed a chequer-board floor and a banister with iron art nouveaux tulip and field mice running up it.

'Jesus,' he hissed. 'Where am I?

'Have you opened your eyes?'

Jani slammed his eyes shut.

'No,' he said.

The next moment he felt a cotton bag being pulled over his head. Then his hands were bound.

'My wallet's in my pocket. Why don't you just take it?' said Jani relatively calmly.

'I don't want it,' said the woman, the voice was losing its disguise.

'Then what do you want?' asked Jani, as terror began to take hold.

'You,' said the voice.

'Don't kill me,' said Jani. 'I'm married.'

The voice laughed.

'What I mean is that I've got children,' pleaded Jani.

'What the fuck difference does that make? They're not tied up with bags over their heads.'

'I'm a father,' said Jani. 'Think how bad things will be for them if anything bad happens to me. I don't care what happens to me. What would they do without me?'

'You're pathetic,' her voice had become recognisable.

'I'm not,' said Jani. 'I just think you should pick on someone single, without children.'

'You didn't say that when you first slept with me,' said the voice.

'It was a mistake,' he said.

'You're pathetic.'

'That was different,' he said.

'Take your clothes off.'

'What?'

Like an old style escapologist Jani began to writhe free from the straight jacket of his clothes.

MONDAY, OCTOBER 28TH

She wasn't there. Niko handed in his human geography essay wondering where in the physical geography was Laura. Nobody had heard or seen of her, at least nobody was owning up to knowing anything. Marko and Snap were truly ignorant. Neither had girlfriends and they tended to regard that part of Niko's life as a grey area. Sabel, the visitor, had no idea about anything, and since her attack she'd become nervous and inattentive; she provided no information.

The other girls, the ones he last spoke to when they were drinking mulled wine, didn't reveal anything. When he asked them about Laura, Jani saw their eyes flashing.

Niko left his class with the distinct impression that Laura was avoiding him.

*   *   *

It was 11.30 am when Jani returned to the bar. He was supposed to be in college but after collecting the homework during the first lesson he realised he couldn't go on. That morning he had woken up tied to a banister in an ornate stair well. His foot, seven steps up, next to an open bottle of bleach, a funnel and an empty bottle of whisky, was pale and bloodless. It was tied to a wrought iron tulip with red bandana with tiny white spots on it. His head, seven steps down, was red, bulging with blood. His eyes, which must have been the size of pool balls, seemed to be rubbing their way out his head. His mouth tasted of whisky, which he guessed had been poured down his throat with a funnel. His clothes were piled yards away in corner. His hands were cuffed to a brass lamp fitting at the base of the staircase. The smell of bleach, oozing up from the marble, made him retch.

Memories of the night swashed around his head like flotsam on a bile green sea of whisky and bleach. Resting a tremulous hand on the bar he ordered a coffee.

'Better put a brandy in that,' said a familiar voice.

It was Smoke. Priest sat by the window behind a newspaper. A voice emerged from behind it.

'I envy you your energy,' said Priest.

Jani did not even have the energy to speak, nor did he have the money to pay for his drink. The fat one, Wisdom, who seemed to have something to do with the barman, created a slate for Jani.

'I can't begin to say what happened,' stammered Jani. 'In a way, I think I was raped, although I can't remember anything.'

'That's shocking,' said Priest. 'But how can you make such an extravagant claim... if you can't remember anything.'

'I dunno,' said Jani. Recalling the humiliating business of asking the concierge to saw through his cuffs earlier that morning.

*   *   *

Janja's apartment was on the tenth floor, close to the top. She watched as the clouds of October mist clinging to the river rolled back. All over the city, buildings seemed to be stepping out of their dressing gowns. She understood what the burning off of seasonal fog meant. Her life had been mistaken. She had created fantasies, lived them, become them. Now they had gone. Today the shutters were all open and the light was pouring in.

She sung as she flitted around the kitchen preparing coffee. Before today the small white table in her kitchen reminded her of a vet's operating table; now it looked different. It was a very optimistic table, she thought, a table built in an era of hope.

As Janja poured her coffee she wondered if she had been depressed. On balance, she decided, she probably had been. How long had she been depressed for? A month? Six months? Two months? Two years? It didn't seem to matter. Because now she felt wonderful, better than ever. She had created this fictitious friend, Gregor, a clueless completely un-scientific policeman. He had left her because he knew that she was feeling better. His role had run out. He didn't hang around waiting for thanks and gifts to get hollowed out. What a perfect man, she thought.

As Janja waited for her coffee to cool, she wondered whether, if Gregor was alive, if he was real, and if he wasn't her, she would have fallen in love with him and not the younger, more handsome specimen, Peter.

As she sipped her coffee, Janja concluded that not being Gregor was actually a great relief. Apart from the fact that the world actually made sense (when Janja was Gregor he never understood why he had to go and lecture undergraduates about molecules), his own preconceptions about the criminal world were relentless. His preoccupation with crime, seeking explanations where perhaps there really were none, ignoring conclusion when they were abundantly clear, infuriated Janja. With Gregor gone, the meaninglessness disappeared. Janja no longer shared this nagging desire to solve some ill-defined, all-encompassing mystery that would bring the biggest case of his life to a satisfactory conclusion. The impossibility of achieving this got her down, it got Gregor down, but, annoyingly, he never stopped trying, even though he seemed to accept the fact that his whole life was a litany of pointless and irrelevant failures. He never gave up. This dogged desire to achieve the impossible, and grumble about it, was the main thing Janja liked about Gregor. She had to admit, having nothing to do with him was a great relief.

'Sorry, Gregor,' she muttered, knowing he'd disapprove.

When Janja left the flat she was already late for her appointment with the Dean.

*   *   *

In his hunting lodge, the Dormouse Master sat on a tree stump writing. He was copying something from one piece of paper to another. So far he had managed to create twenty seven questionnaires.

*   *   *

The Dean himself was a man of gravitas. At sixty he gave the impression of even greater age. His lumpy sports jacket, his half-moon spectacles, his crumpled face, his neat tie, his woolly hair, his collection of cheap biros, his notebook, his eyebrows, all gave him the appearance of inner brilliance hidden by the dusters he used to polish it. It was hard to imagine such a man at say – seventeen: thin, scrawny, uncertain, foolish. The Dean had striven for years to overlay his original, rather tentative self with a druidic persona. The only weaknesses he was prepared to admit to now were a predilection for Irish whisky and a tendency to smoke in the street in moments of stress. He raised his eyebrows high and peered across his desk at Janja, sitting in a big uncomfortable oak chair before him.

'Run that by me again?' he said, looking perplexed.

Janja smiled nervously, she'd just been trying to explain her concerns to the Dean. How she hadn't been fully engaged with her lab work because she thought she was a police officer, or more accurately, an ex-cop, private detective who had no crimes to solve. How she had long felt boxed in by her career. How she sometimes believed that the science she did wasn't really very open minded, because she was never able to follow her own lines of enquiry because she took direction from, amongst others, the Dean, who was himself subject to the whims of the University Statutory Committee, who themselves were simply in it for as much money as they get from whoever they thought might have some. How she had feelings of guilt about this – as if it was a sin. How, occasionally, it seemed to her that her primary function was to pitch for contracts for research projects into uninteresting subjects which had little or no scientific value, whilst the real story festered in her head, turning sour, dying of old age. How she felt like a 'yes' woman. How, when someone asked Gregor whether Charles Darwin or someone else discovered evolution, he just said 'hmmm, it's an idea' and talked about something else. How she liked that, not because it was right but because it was different.

'The thing you have to do,' said Janja, leaning earnestly towards the Dean's desk, 'is not to ask yourself: 'how much money', or: 'is there an application', or even: 'could I get funding for this'. A simple 'how' will suffice. When you have enough answers to 'how', you may create a big enough pile to tip the balance for a 'why'. Perhaps that's the way our minds work. On one level, we are all no more than beef stew with structure. But how many bowls of stew do you know that can explode atom bombs or make Ray Bans? Find out how it works and perhaps we will understand why. We learn tiny amounts through incredibly small steps – we're not as smart as we think we are.'

The Dean held up his hand as Janja rambled over some of the other points she'd already made.

'Please, don't,' he said. 'I have one or two questions of my own. To be honest, I'm not sure I need a lecture from you about anything.'

Janja nodded.

'Are you seeing Gregor now?'

'No.'

'And he's the one who doesn't exist?'

'Yes.'

'Good, no problem. Thank you very much Janja, I look forward to reading that paper you're writing on cross cellular energy transference in GM potatoes – there's a lot of interest in your work, Janja.'

Janja lingered in the chair for a moment. Then, with a shrug, she stood up.

'Thank you,' she said.

*　*　*

The irony of the situation was lost, or, at least, ignored by Slabo. Vala watched from the shadows at the back of the room, where plastic seats had been stacked and hidden behind some grey curtains. They were roped and gathered up a few centimetres above the floor and they billowed over her, like clouds. Vala's long dark dress merged with the curtains, making her almost invisible, although occasionally, her face, which was pale, almost stony, would twitch, signalling her position. Perhaps she was more like a statue than a cloud, the kind you find in serious gardens: a concrete muse perched on a patio chair - except this one had red lips which quivered whenever Slabo said something hypocritical.

'We can, I believe, with a spirit of cooperation and vigilance, drive the criminal element from our society. Of course there will always be crime, but I think it is fair to say that the goal of creating a safe environment for our children, where the streets are safe and public standards of behaviour are high, is not impossible. We can stop crime, we will stop crime, we must stop crime but it is up to each and every one of us to play our part.'

The audience clapped. A few photographers snapped as Slabo smiled broadly, lifting his hand to acknowledge the applause before stepping down off the low stage to speak, in more detail, with the journalists. As he chatted, he moved towards the table laden with the finger buffet, leading the way for the other delegates. He extended two fingers and expertly selected a chicken goujon, removing it without disturbing the teetering tower of legs and wings with surgical precision. As he ate, he handed out sound bites, like sweets to hungry orphans.

Vala watched and listened: she had become architectural.

As Slabo's fingers lifted a small water biscuit to his mouth, so the thirty or so delegates drawn from the government's law enforcement agencies, trading standards departments and the police and security departments, followed suit; shifting and picking around the tables, nibbling effectively and speaking quietly so that they could overhear as much as possible.

'Naturally street lighting will be improved,' said Slabo. 'Some parts of town have no adequate lighting at all. Indeed, I have made several unofficial sorties into the less reputable parts of our city in the early hours and I can confirm that they are unacceptably dark. Light must be a key factor in repelling criminals.'

He took a prawn from a starburst of prawns.

'Take the Black Forest,' added Slabo. 'I must confess that I felt extremely unsafe in those dark streets; those people who live there are blighted by an environment of fear and hostility. First I say: 'let there be light'. Then when we can see the perpetrators; I say: 'let there be justice."

He reached for a chive and salmon blini.

'And let justice be done, be seen to be done, and be actually done.'

And a biscuit size anchovy and caper pizza.

'I want to send a personal message out to anyone who is thinking of committing a crime tonight. Don't do it. We will see you. We will seek you. We will punish you.'

And then a tiny lamb and mushroom kofta.

'So our first priority is efficient lighting, then more surveillance cameras and also more police. But the public must join in and play their part in the partnership.'

And then Slabo spotted something that he had not seen for some time. He would have to lean over a tureen of pumpkin and sour cream soup to reach it. The platter he was aiming at was almost empty. A local delicacy, rarely seen on the trestles of corporate finger buffets, like a relic from another time, at the rim of its lunar plate. It was a roasted dormouse. Slabo watched it, trying to subdue his excitement, praying that nobody else made a grab for it.

'If you, and I mean you, and me, and everyone – I mean 'us' - sees a crime being perpetuated. We must not be afraid to step in. Don't hold back and leave the responsibility to someone else. Take the initiative. Apprehend the miscreants. Call the police.'

The dormouse reminded Slabo of summer holidays at his uncle's farm. He could already taste the little creature. He felt as if he was still there, at the farm, helping with the harvest, maybe forty years ago. He felt as if none of the events that populated his life had actually occurred. It was as if the finger buffet, like everything else, was just a day dream, lodged between bales of hay. He felt as if his uncle was still alive and that he was helping with the grape picking. Slabo lunged across the table and swept up the dormouse – the connection. Holding the little creature between his fingers he felt as if all his troubles were blowing away. The simplest cure for homesickness is always the same. Now Slabo felt as if the dormouse was actually a much more significant relic, like a splinter from the true cross, or one of St James' bones.

'Perhaps it's a good time to announce another aspect of our policy. As of today a new government hotline is being opened. The Crime Line – call if you see a crime, if you are a victim of crime, or if you feel that you know a crime is taking place. It is up to us all. We want to hear from you,' said Slabo.

The journalists were happy with this. Slabo popped the mouse into his mouth. Waves of nostalgia filled his body. He was transported back to a much happier time. God it tasted good.

Vala sighed. Slabo's ability to capitalise on his own shortcomings always made a strong impression on her. This was a vintage performance. Cloaking his own nocturnal wanderings in the purple toga of public spiritedness typified their problem. For Slabo there was no cloak, at any given moment he believed everything he told himself; for her, there was nothing to believe – everything had to be concocted, order did not occur, it had to be manufactured and held together.

TUESDAY, OCTOBER 29TH

Niko ambled along the pavement next to the big dual carriageway past the National Art Gallery and away. He padded along, his trainers skimming the concrete so that each step made two beats. He was in no particular hurry, it was a familiar route and when he arrived at Laura's, he was sure of something nice to eat. He wandered down into the subway tapping his path beneath the dual carriageway, emerging on the other side into a different world. Allotments sailed under high bamboo structures laden with beans as long as swords; tomato plants bent under the weight of their last offerings; orange pumpkins burst from the soil; marrows spread on the ground, their leaves completely masking the earth. Niko sauntered through the exploding earth, past ornamental gardens, neat little Swiss rockeries, riotous nasturtiums fleeing their pots, orderly piles of courgettes and leeks, and, hanging like drops of caramel from their wilting leaves, over-ripe grapes for bees to eat. Here the air was thick with insects, bonfire smoke and the sound of chain saws.

Laura lived in a large half-timbered bungalow with a stone chimney running up the gable end. The architect couple who lived next door had attached a metal and glass cone to their house; within it was a circular staircase screwing upwards to a roof garden. Opposite, an empty swimming pool collected autumn leaves in front of a wedding cake white house complete with Corinthian columns and acanthus flowers. Niko liked Laura's neighbourhood, the mish-mash nature of the place was a refreshing alternative to his own stand of well-organised tower blocks. A few years back, an earthquake had struck, causing some of the dominant structures in Laura's suburb to collapse, their replacements added to the 'free range' feel. The place had a sunny Mediterranean feel, the gardens contained palm trees and cedars as well as apples and the occasional oak. The streets were sandy and orange coloured and people barbecued sardines in their back gardens in summer.

It wasn't the Mediterranean though. As Niko turned the corner into Laura's drive, he knew that they had a few hours peace and quiet before everyone returned from work. People who lived in Laura's area were professionals who lived life by the clock. It was hard to believe, but at 17.30, every day, they made their own traffic jam. As he pressed the door bell and the familiar tune rang inside he wondered where, exactly, Laura had been.

There was no answer.

Niko rang again.

The bell chimed inside.

Niko looked around. A couple of swallows hurtled past.

Niko walked back down Laura's short drive and sat on the low brick wall, the boundary between Laura's place and the road. He was getting worried. It was most unlike Laura to disappear. She was a compulsive communicator, her mobile, her online sites, were always a hive of chatter. But Niko had seen and heard nothing since that night at the concert, when he didn't see her. His own phone wasn't working at that moment, he'd lost the charger, but when it was full of juice, she didn't answer. The nagging feeling that something was wrong began to invade Niko.

Niko went back to the door bell and pressed it.

After a tiny delay, it chimed out its unrequited tune, the first few bars of a famous old symphony.

Now, Niko felt worried. What had happened to Laura? He shouted, he walked around the back of her house, peering through the windows. The place looked neat and tidy, there were no coffee cups on the kitchen table. There was nobody about.

Niko decided to wait. He returned to his wall and encouraged his mind to come up with scenarios: things Laura might be doing which would explain why she had disappeared so completely from public view. There weren't very many.

A small blue car burbled into the street. Niko stood up, it was Laura's mother. This was strange. Laura's mother worked in a school, she was never around in the afternoon. The car drew to a halt and with a cheery wave Laura's mother stepped out, carrying her briefcase and a plastic bag full of shopping.

'Where is she?' asked Niko.

'Who,' asked Laura's mother, preoccupied as she handed Niko the bag of shopping so that she could carry an armful of files from the car to her house.

'Laura,' said Niko.

'I think you'd better come in for a cup of coffee,' said Laura's mum, fumbling for the house key.

*   *   *

Before Janja had stopped seeing her friends she thought that they were selfish. Her relationship with them had become a kind of formal dance with strict rules, which she felt eviscerated any possibility of doing anything interesting. Janja came to the conclusion that friendship, indeed, social interactions of any kind, had been misrepresented and misunderstood. When she deconstructed her relationships with others, she found that all of her presuppositions about what friendship meant, what relationships were, and even, in the end, just talking, had no substance. Once upon a time Janja had liked her friends, but, as the true nature of things became manifest, she realised that the main reason, the only reason, why anybody spoke to her, was to let her know how clever they thought they were. In a sense, Janja came to see a dialogue as a monologue. The exchange had no value other than to shore up the egos of frightened people who needed to broadcast in order to maintain the illusion of their own autonomy.

Before falling silent Janja tried to placate herself with the theory that a conversation had some use. It was an exchange or a transaction, a bargain or a deal. It enabled trade in things and ideas. Talking, if not beautiful, was utilitarian. Janja was entitled to tell her friends about her problems, fixations and hang-ups, and to receive earnest, optimistic advice on the understanding that she reciprocated. But even this colourless line didn't hold for long. Conversation for Janja became two monologues, a pointless exchange, like the sound of two birds from different species chirping together in the same tree. Before she stopped talking altogether Janja still believed her friends really were trying to help her. But as time passed and her own problems grew, Janja felt that their preoccupations seemed increasingly trivial when compared with her own dark feelings of foreboding. First Janja stopped listening, then she stopped talking, after that she stopped seeing her friends. Looking back, she felt a little guilty about her behaviour. She'd been very selfish, replacing dialogue, with monologue then, eventually, with her own unique nonologue.[4]

After not speaking to anyone for a while, Janja realised that she was becoming insular. That was when she started going to see a shrink. The shrink gave Janja the impression that her problems were her own fault. That they didn't come from the exterior world and her old boyfriend, Peter, was not at the bottom of it all. Somehow, said the shrink, the difficulties had built up inside her and she was their architect. The shrink suggested that they stemmed from the way she had grown, from her family, her school, her environment, even the house they used to visit during the summer holidays.

---

4. *This is a neologism.*

'Buildings are the worst,' the shrink would say. 'They are the sentences and paragraphs of architects – all of whom are delusional fantasists. I know because architects make up a significant number of my clients.'

The shrink claimed that everything that Janja had perceived on the outside had been incorrectly rebuilt inside her. The problem was that the foundations of many of Janja's internal buildings were faulty and they had to excavate the recesses of her mind and memory to put things right. For a time, somewhat reluctantly, Janja went along with her analyst's obsession with buildings. Then a neighbour's cat got run over by a bus, throwing its owner into a deep depression. Why, she thought, does sadness have to be solvable? The cat's death was not some story. It was real. It happened outside, only a few yards away from the Dragon Bridge. And it made everyone sad. Might not being miserable be a perfectly reasonable state to be in? After all, if your cat was run over wouldn't you feel sad? Scientifically speaking, might feeling sad actually be the most appropriate emotional state for a human being to occupy? Surely, reasoned Janja, the delusional ones are the happy ones. She stopped going to the shrink and didn't say much to anyone. That was when she came across Gregor.

Today, Janja felt happy. She'd arranged to meet an old friend, someone she hadn't seen for months, or maybe years, at a cafe.

Natalie and Janja sat outside the cafe next to the clever three spanned bridge with its complicated pedestrian walkways, in the shadow of the church, on the opposite side of the river to the colonnaded market where the pumpkin seller had stacked up his display of carved pumpkins, each containing a flickering candle. The scent of charred pumpkin gave the air an almost toasty bite. It was chilly in the shade. They both wore thick coats.

'I have,' announced Natalie, who wore a bright red shawl and was prone to making dramatic statements, 'turned to reading.'

She flicked her voluminous black hair back, her red nails flashing in the sunlight.

'Really,' said Janja, imperceptibly analysing the pedestrians walking across the bridge opposite.

If he was anywhere, he would be there, watching.

'There's so much in literature. Honestly, I think every problem, every situation, every possible twist and turn you could imagine has been explored in some book or other,' said Natalie. 'I like Hardy and Dostoevsky at the moment.'

'Really,' said Janja.

'Sometimes I feel as if,' Natalie paused, her brown eyes flashed around the buildings surrounding them, as if seeking inspiration. She pointed at a woman throwing bread into the river for the ducks, 'that, really is me.'

'What?' asked Janja.

'That woman there, or that one there, or that one over there, they are all doing things that authors have explained. It's reassuring to know that you're not alone.'

Janja sipped her lemonade.

'I love reading so much. I don't know, it's quite hard to express how much better I feel after I have seen some aspect of myself in a book, do you know what I mean?'

Janja nodded. She knew what Gregor would say: 'Hmmm, a story?'

She couldn't help smiling. So as not to look rude, Janja spoke.

'Do you know,' she said , 'that although I have the power to grow a potato the size of a pumpkin, using techniques of genetic modification, I cannot tell you why plants are green, some say they should be black.'

Natalie looked at Janja in confusion. She couldn't tell whether Janja was joking or not. The last Natalie had heard of Janja was that she had gone crazy.

'I'm talking about my life here,' persisted Natalie, without much conviction. 'I feel like 'Tess of the D'Urbervilles.'

'Well you're not are you? You weren't raped by a landlord and you haven't killed anybody. The only thing you and Tess have in common is that you married an arse. So you don't need to worry about that,' said Janja finishing her lemonade. 'You know what I think?'

'No,' said Natalie.

'I think you should stop living with that stupid airhead husband of yours.'

Natalie looked hurt.

'We got divorced last year,' she said. 'I was coming to that bit.'

'I'm sorry,' said Janja.

Things improved.

* * *

'Each bullet is carefully selected, weighed, filed, balanced, polished so that it travels through the air like light, not a stone age projectile. The gun is stripped, cleaned, nurtured, so that its mechanical parts mesh together with the precision of a chronometer. The lenses in the sights are contained in a sealed, dust-free environment. The stock is balanced with tiny particles of lead. The first element in the art of killing is technological. The essence of technology is precision. Without precision nothing works. Technology is the art of work.'

Zebedee muttered these words as he polished the bullet he had chosen – a little gold capsule. He looked at the reflection of his nose on the surface of the bullet. It reminded him of the doorknobs in his grandmother's house.

'I have isolated the target,' he muttered.

*　　*　　*

Clara was conscious of the fact that she was being watched – she rather liked it. Instead of catching the bus straight from the depot to her place, she had decided to have a drink in one of the more expensive bars in town on the way home. She was sitting on a bar-stool, dressed in her coat and boots, with her make up on and her bus company uniform crammed into a plastic bag on the floor at the base of her stool. The man, who'd arrived after her, said hello and offered to buy Clara a drink. She declined. But she spoke to him. She rather liked the fact that she was, if not the centre of attention, the object of some attention. A few other of the male occupants of the bar, all wearing suits, were giving her sly glances.

It turned out that Clara's fellow was an engineer. He worked just around the corner. He was thirty one years old. He had worked abroad, in Germany and Sweden, and he was almost famous. In his teens he had been in the national skiing team. But he broke a leg and never regained the same speed, or, as Clara gently pointed out, recklessness. Clara liked his eyes, light blue, like pebbles in a mountain stream, she thought. He was very easy to be with, quiet, but not boring; full of interesting stories told in a matter-of-fact almost serious way. Better still, he didn't ask questions – nothing about her job, her family, whether she was married or not. She, on the other hand, knew that Steiner was single, that he had almost got married once, when he lived in Stockholm, that he had two brothers and three sisters, that his mother was a poet and his father was a maths teacher and they didn't speak to one another.

When it was time for Clara to leave - she had to pick her son up from her mother's place - Steiner gave her his card and asked to her to keep in touch. He asked her for her number too. Clara gave him the details and accepted his card. She told Steiner that she was called Janja, just to be on the safe side.

As she walked home, Clara was surprised at her reaction to such an inconsequential little meeting. Perhaps it was not so trivial. For the last three years, since the departure of her husband, she'd barely had a conversation with a man on any subject beyond bus rosters and hydraulic doors. It was the first time she'd been into a bar on her own for more than three years, seven years, perhaps, maybe ten years and look what had happened. Did it simply take a couple of glasses of beer in some swanky bar to find a really interesting, handsome, young man? No, she answered the question herself, the magic ingredients were her clothes, her coat and the boots and everything that came with them. With this look she could do anything she wanted. The new clothes made her interesting, attractive and sexy. The old ones, in the plastic bag swinging by her side, were their antidote. She watched her reflection sweeping along the street in every available shop window. Perhaps she could have had sex with Steiner, not that she wanted to. She stopped and considered her reflection. On reflection, maybe she did.

A bus pulled up behind her. The driver whistled.

Clara grinned. All he could see was her back. She decided not to turn around.

*　　*　　*

Niko had followed Laura's mother into her house. She led the way to the kitchen and offered him some instant coffee. As he helped unpack the shopping he asked about Laura. But he couldn't get straight answers. Her mother just talked about her day – teaching, shopping and, like Niko, wondering where the hell her daughter was.

'She's fine, she's just in one of those teenage moods, you know, she says she needs to be alone.'

'So where is she?'

'Alone, I guess.'

'Is that good?

'It's what she wants,'

'Do you know where she is?'

'No.'

'Where is she now?

'I told you, I don't know, she's being alone.'

'Where, where is she alone?'

'With a friend.'

It took Niko a moment or two to think.

'What kind of a friend?'

'I don't know, not a serious kind of friend.'

Niko was getting angry.

'Can I get you another coffee?' asked Laura's mother.

'Where exactly is Laura, who precisely is she with and what, in a nutshell, is she doing?'

'Would you like a pizza?' asked Laura's mother. 'I'm going to have one.'

'Yes but where's Laura?'

Laura's mother put a friendly hand on Niko's shoulder. She squeezed it.

*   *   *

After an enjoyable hour with Natalie, Janja had spent the rest of the day shopping. Gregor never bought clothes, he just hung around in public libraries or stayed at home. Janja, who had previously disapproved of shopping, now delighted in it. She wandered through the stores soaking in their cosmopolitan devil-may-care optimism. Previously, even before she was depressed, she'd railed against the commodification of society through the proliferation of off-the-peg thrills. Now she understood: lipstick, something which previously tasted of gender politics, simply looked alluring; shoes attracted her and clothes changed her mood. Janja bought what she wanted, why couldn't she look as good as Natalie? She shopped and bought herself countless coffees, pushed her new sunglasses up and then let them fall low over her nose. The world was full of toys.

By eight o'clock Janja was tired. She walked into a busy bar for a drink. As she entered the room, a striking-looking woman wearing a long black coat swept past her. The man she had left behind watched her with, as Janja saw it, a rueful smile. She did not recognise the man, but she thought she knew the type. Successful, professional, he probably worked in an office completely unlike her laboratory. It would be dustless, paperless, bookless and glassy, smelling of air fresheners rather than formaldehyde, with wafer-thin computer screens and deep leather chairs. She sat next to him and ordered herself a Martini, a drink she had never tried before.

The man smiled at her.

'What's so funny?' asked Janja, allowing her shopping bags to fall to the floor around her.

'Nothing,' said the man, sticking his leg out to stop one of the bags from toppling over.

'Then why are you laughing?' asked Janja.

'I'm sorry,' said the man, 'it's just that I've been coming to this bar for some time now, and never have I fallen into conversations with so many beautiful women.'

'Does that include me?' asked Janja, peering over the top of her sunglasses. 'I'd hardly call this a conversation, I don't really think we're actually speaking. Do you?'

'I'm sure we definitely are.'

Janja chinked her glass against the man's.

'Cheers,' she said. 'I never come here. In fact, I very rarely go out. I've been shopping.'

The man nodded, looking at the range of bags on the floor.

'Clearly,' he smiled. 'I'm Steiner.'

Janja nodded, sipping her drink, she didn't want to stand out.

'I'm Clara,' she said.

It was on this night that the Dormouse Master finished his work in the forest. For several days he had slept in his hunting lodge. By night he uprooted pine trees. Now, the owls could see that the starlit work was almost done.

The Dormouse Master addressed one last pine tree, embracing it in his arms and pulling with all his might. The thin soil relented and the Dormouse Master took the strain, rising upwards almost as if he was becoming weightless, floating up into the air, struggling to keep his balance as the huge pine tree rose slowly, like a space rocket, upwards from it gantry. The Dormouse Master staggered to the side of the clearing, his tree moved, as if it had sprouted legs, through the forest canopy. When they reached the space, the Dormouse Master allowed the tree to crash down onto a pile of around thirty others. He slapped his hands together, dislodging the pine needles, bark and earth that stuck into his skin.

He spat with satisfaction, surveying the clearing he'd made: a corridor in the forest, joining a network of dark passages. Across the whole hillside there were more paths with felled trees strewn around as if uprooted by an elephant escaped from a circus. The Dormouse Master had finished his work. He knew that what he had created could not be equalled.

He made his way down the slope towards the opposite side of the valley. This was one sunrise he didn't want to miss.

WEDNESDAY, OCTOBER 30TH

At the same time, well after midnight, Niko left Laura's mother's house. The front door clicked closed and he found himself stumbling back down the path. By the time he had reached the street, which was quite dark because the streetlights weren't working, he was almost shaking with anger. He was drunk, he had been seduced and compromised. When he reached the second gloomy lamp post, Niko's anger had matured into self-loathing. How could the things that had just happened have happened? Instead of finding out the truth about his girlfriend, instead of learning that she'd run off with someone else, he'd fucked her mother. Niko swayed erratically towards the distant dual carriageway. Now he was the villain of the piece and he still knew nothing. Laura's mother hadn't told him where Laura was, or who she was with. Either Laura's mother or Laura had lied to him. Or maybe they were both in it together. But why? Why pick on him? Niko let out a cry. It echoed under the motorway, reverberating off the sides of the subway. If Laura had simply finished with him he'd have had no cause to visit her house. If she'd levelled with him he'd have been fine. Now, because Laura had refused to speak he was right up to his neck in it. Should he tell her what had happened, or should he pretend everything was OK and hope that her mother didn't spill the beans? Niko stumbled through the subway and onto the road leading to the Dragon Bridge. The riverbank was quiet. The willow branches hung like cobwebs in starlight. A few fishermen sat like black gnomes on the riverbank, their long rods disappearing over the deep black water.

Niko weaved his way forwards muttering to himself. It was all her fault. If she'd had the guts to tell him what was going on he would never had had to call around. He would never have accepted the pizza, the wine, the tequila. Everything was spinning. He threw up on the grass near the little humpback bridge.

A man scurried towards him, he was coming from the direction of town and the Dragon Bridge. He was slight and he moved with the speed of a rat.

'Oh fuck,' muttered Niko, instantly recognising his old assailant.

Instinctively, Niko foraged in his pockets to see if he had any cash at all, knowing that he would come up empty handed. But the man didn't see him, or he chose to ignore him. He tumbled off along the river bank, sometimes on all fours, occasionally glancing backwards. Sensing something was amiss, if that is the right way to describe not being mugged, Niko crouched down just next to the spot where he'd vomited.

Another man appeared. He seemed more organised. He didn't run. He moved with the speed and silence of a soldier, sliding along the riverbank. Niko could see that the new man was clothed entirely in black, from his balaclava to his shoes. He stopped and produced something from his coat. Niko looked on in horror as the man shouldered a rifle with a telescopic sight and silencer. He watched the man steady himself, aim and fire. Niko, without moving his head, tried to revolve his eyes so that he could see if anybody'd been hit. There was no noise. Nothing moved. Then he heard it. Unmistakable – splash.

The balaclava man slipped away disappearing into the unlit sector from which Niko had emerged.

Niko hardly dared to breathe. He remained exactly in the same position.

* * *

Zebedee performed his favourite trick. He disappeared like a patch of gas. He had harvested another life from his garden of misdemeanours.

Janja stepped out of the shower wearing Steiner's bathrobe. It reached her feet. They stuck out from the thick white towelling, nestling into the woollen carpet like two little hot dogs surrounded by soft bread. Steiner sat at the kitchen table eating muesli, two cups of coffee stood steaming on the table.

'Nice flat,' said Janja, admiring the glass, the chrome, the black marble, the expensive cooking utensils, the multiplicity of shower nozzles, the deep rugs, the balcony, the computer screens, the tablets, the gorgeous bed and the generally dust-free, well-organised nature of things.

'Thanks,' said Steiner.

'It's yours?' asked Janja.

'The company pays, I chose it though. I wanted something functional and comfortable,' he smiled at Janja pushing a cup of coffee towards her.

'My place is in the country,' said Steiner. 'It's much more bucolic there, perhaps you'd like to visit it.'

Janja looked a little embarrassed. Screwing the stranger, Steiner, in the company apartment was one thing, visiting his house, which might contain dust and books, was another – they might not get on.

'It's beautiful,' said Steiner.

'I'm sure it is,' said Janja.

'I'd love to show it to you, Clara,' said Steiner.

'Thank you, that would be lovely,' said Janja, 'I'll just go and get dressed.'

As she changed, Janja reviewed the situation. She was in a stranger's flat, putting on different, new clothes, pretending to be someone called Clara and she felt great. She wished she'd spent more time in bars picking up guys like Steiner. He was a pleasure to be with – funny, intelligent, kind yet at the same time, reassuringly disinterested in the details of her life. He was also a good fuck.

'Will I see you again?' asked Steiner.

Janja grinned at him, 'maybe'.

She kissed him on the lips.

Janja walked down the stairs of his apartment block, into the hallway. She noticed its wrought iron banister shaped into tulips with field mice chasing up and down the stairs, its chequer-board floor tiles, dry flowers and lingering smell of lemon scented cleaning fluid. She pushed the heavy old door open and emerged onto a busy street near the old Dragon Bridge. The air, full of the soft scents of autumn and the particulate remains of city life, flooded her senses.

* * *

Nearby, on the bank of the river, a few meters away from Niko's sick, Slabo was finishing a TV interview.

'This was a cynical murder,' he was saying. 'An innocent man, a fisherman, gunned down for no reason, whilst pursuing his harmless past-time. If we can learn anything from this senseless crime we can appreciate this. We must act as a community. We must work together to bring the psychopath who did this to justice.'

'Would you say that the streets of our city are unsafe?' asked the interviewer.

'No I would not, not if we are vigilant. Only yesterday I announced a number of measures designed to make this more possible. It is just regrettable that it takes an event like this to bring the importance of what I say home to us all. I note that this section of the river, for example, is extremely badly lit. I promise to ensure that the standard of lighting will improve drastically.'

'There is talk,' said the journalist, 'of a river bank mugger. Someone who preys on innocent victims along the waterfront and is not afraid to kill for little reward. Do you think there is a connection between the activities we are seeing in this sector?'

'I've heard the rumours, about a Troll Man who lives under the bridge,' said Slabo. 'It's nothing but seasonal gossip. We're approaching Halloween and people have over-active imaginations. This crime, whilst despicable, is not extraordinary, it isn't supernatural, it isn't pre-meditated; it is an isolated incident.'

'The fisherman had apparently been fishing this stretch of the river for many years. What can you say to reassure the others who fish at nights along the banks of the river?'

'I don't think we're talking about a vendetta here. It is even possible that the killer mistook the fisherman for someone else.'

'Another reason for better lighting,' said the journalist gravely. She turned to the camera and began her link to the studio.

Vala watched from the car. The police strutted, spreading plastic tape and signs around the river bank. A well-dressed young inspector, wearing a long coat and striking tie, dictated instructions to a uniformed offer. He was opening up all the usual lines of enquiry. Who was the fisherman? Did he have any enemies? Were there any family members who hated him? Jealous colleagues at work? Rivals at the fishing club? He spoke loudly, he wanted everyone to hear. His eyes flicked around the scene – he was searching for the two officers who had first discovered the body.

Vala studied him carefully. She tried to push Slabo's rhetoric out of her ears as the inspector hurried to his men. The inspector spoke forcefully, but quietly, to the two uniformed men who'd found the body.

'Where's the fucking fishing rod, the guy's torch, his keep net – even his fucking fish?'

The men shrugged.

'Must have fallen in the river, Sir,' one of them said.

The inspector looked across at Slabo and the press.

'I'll be visiting the market – I'll be on the look-out for second hand tackle. If I find any, you two will be patrolling this river for the rest of your careers.'

Slabo walked thoughtfully towards his car, pausing to be photographed next to the bouquets of flowers that had been positioned near the riverbank, where the body had become trapped in a whirlpool. Slabo adopted a solemn, resolute visage; he listened as the cameras clicked. As soon as he could he hurried into his car where Vala sat, pushing down the quicks of her nails.

'Take me to the old barracks, bitch,' he yelled.

Vala gave him a cold, lifeless stare, before accelerating off.

*　*　*

What with the pumpkin soup, the near misses with the weirdo from under the bridge, a disastrous mark for his integrated transport essay, the disappearance of his girlfriend and his sexual relationship with her mother, Niko had a lot on his mind. His drunken stumble along the riverbank had left yet more uncertainty.

Doubts concerning his own perceptions and the reliability of the cops, who would remember him from his last visit, prevented Niko from presenting himself at a police station, as the reporters on the television suggested he should. Niko didn't trust the police or himself and he couldn't sleep.

He had begun to jog to tire himself out. Anything less than 5K per day had no effect, but if he managed more, he was assured of a reasonably sound sleep free of confused images of pizzas, busses, muggers and pumpkins. Only the rhythm of his trainers, tapping on the concrete, helped gather his thoughts.

After a few days he resolved to revisit the crime scene and try to see for himself what had happened. One evening he, Marko and Snap returned to the river. The area was still cordoned off with tape left by the police. They wandered over the site, trying to piece together the events of the evening. Marko picked up a blade of grass. He scrutinized it.

'If only this grass could talk,' he said.

Snap sat down on the riverbank, watching the water.

'The more you look at it, the spookier it gets,' he said. 'It kind of sucks things down.'

Niko paced between the other two.

'You were pissed, you'd just thrown up, you'd shagged Laura's mother, your mind was playing tricks on you,' said Marko.

'I know I saw something,' said Niko. 'It's just very hazy. I couldn't swear by any of it.'

'What was it like?' asked Snap.

'Fucking weird, he moved so quickly, but at the same time he was kind of … slow.'

'I mean with Laura's mother,' said Niko. 'I've never been with an older woman. Was she really hot?'

'She was trying to mess my with mind,' said Niko.

'Oh,' said Marko.

'Of course she was hot,' said Niko. The truth was she was so hot that the jogging therapy was losing its potency. She was the real reason he couldn't sleep.

'Wow,' said Snap.

'You going to see her again?' asked Marko.

'I can't,' said Niko.

'Why not?' asked Snap.

'Because of Laura,' said Niko. 'It would be too fucked up and weird.'

'That's no reason not to go back,' said Marko.

'I don't want to,' said Niko.

'Would you like me to talk to her?' asked Marko.

'That won't be necessary,' said Niko.

He wandered towards the riverbank.

'Splash,' he shouted, 'and some poor fisherman topples in. He was shot. I saw the guy who shot him. I'm sure I didn't dream it. I'd only just thrown up. It's Laura's fault, well her mother's. I don't know what to do. I feel like I'm going nuts.'

'You could take Sabel out,' said Snap. 'She likes you, she thinks you saved her life.'

'Yeah,' said Marko, 'it might help you get back to normal. Go on a date.'

*   *   *

Sabel and Niko met at Luigi's, an Italian restaurant popular among students with no money. If customers visit before seven they get ten percent off freshwater fish. So Niko and Sabel ordered crayfish soup followed by trout pizzas. In the orange light from the pumpkin lanterns the place was both low-lit and strange-smelling. It was unromantic. Perhaps a little like hell.

Since she'd come out of her coma Niko hadn't paid much attention to Sabel. He found her gratitude and adoration off-putting and a little embarrassing. But now, faced with the devil woman the other side of the bridge, gnawing at his mind, pulling him back towards her little bungalow in a pumpkin filled suburb, he was ready to try anything. Sabel had been delighted to take up his offer of a visit to Luigi's.

Sabel spoke at length about how all of her family were grateful to Niko. Niko had to do little else but listen and eat.

The meal was pleasant enough and, in the candle light, Niko thought that Sabel looked very pretty. She was polite and earnest and she continually stressed how grateful she was to Niko for standing his ground and saving her life. The light flickered through pumpkin teeth across her round face, her brown eyes seemed to twinkle when she spoke about Niko's bravery, but try as he might, Niko couldn't make himself find her attractive. He tried closing one eye, he tried looking at her from different angles. No matter which direction he approached her from, she wasn't sexy – not for Niko, anyway. He found her puddingy. Her lips were red like raspberries, her skin was creamy like custard, her eyes, dark profiteroles, her golden-brown hair was like candyfloss. She was, Niko thought, too like a mother, all biscuity and cakey, as if she'd just stepped out of a ginger bread house or a cuckoo clock. She, on the other hand, adored every inch of Niko, the hero. Which somehow made things even worse.

When Sabel paid, Niko looked up into the wooden rafters of the restaurant. He saw toy witches riding broomsticks that had been hung from threads.

* * *

A single light glowed yellow in the facade of the ministerial building. From the ground it was only just possible to discern the shapes of Slabo and Vala, staring out. They stood side by side each holding stiff drinks, gazing across the town at the tops of the turrets of the castle. The spotlights shining up the hill gave the ramparts a theatrical, melodramatic air.

'Pretty isn't it,' said Vala.

'Still a bit dark,' said Slabo. 'We're way behind with the 'light the night' campaign.'

'I can see the river,' said Vala. 'It's black. I can see it because I can't see it.'

'It's not lit properly.'

'You put a notice in the barracks?'

'I did.'

'What did it say?' asked Vala. She followed the black gap of the river with her eyes. It was like tracing the course of a wound across a body. It seemed to Vala that the river was like a gash in the silvery, speckled skin of the city. With some relief, her gaze reached the old Dragon Bridge. That was lit up, like the castle, for the tourists. Her eyes, scouring the stanchions of the bridge. What a precocious old bridge. Like an old lady in the bath. With her dragons like jewels. How ostentatious!

'Is it right to wear jewellery in the bath?' she asked.

Slabo looked at Vala.

Vala shook her head.

'It's no good, I'm catching bullshit from you.'

'You don't catch bullshit – you buy it,' said Slabo.

'I think we'll be moving away from this little mess quite quickly,' said Slabo, with confidence.

Vala shuddered. Then she remembered something from her old geography lessons at school. A few kilometres out of town the river disappears, flowing through a system of caves, re-emerging in the plains. When she was sixteen they'd gone to visit the Devil's Mouth, as the cave was called, as part of a school field trip. The image of all that water pouring down into the ground in an everlasting gulp came back to Vala. She remembered thinking, as she leant on the barrier with her classmates, that it was as if the river was being eaten by the earth, although it could never satisfy its appetite. She recalled the spray rising up in clouds of tiny droplets, cooling her skin. She saw trails of sodden mosses dangling down from the roof of the cave, like bits of food around a real mouth. She remembered standing by the hole in the ground, mesmerised by the crash of the water and the unfathomable depth, and the frightening feeling that she could join the water tumbling downwards for ever, simply by stepping over the barrier and letting go. An eternity of tumbling seemed only half a footstep away.

'Are you OK?' said Slabo.

Vala gulped her whisky. Somehow, she concluded, the madness Slabo was suffering from had infected her. She was becoming as detached and introspective as he was, mimicking his self-obsession. She shook herself. She'd spent too many days with Slabo and now she was drifting off into the same dream world as his - where policies worked, and trolls lived under bridges.

'I'm fine,' she said. 'I'm just anxious to move on, maybe to another department.'

The newspapers, everyone she met, seemed to be infected. The talk was of the Troll Man who lived under the bridge, slithering out at night to kill innocent river watchers. It was crazy. Vala shivered – all these deaths.

'I pinned a note on the green baize in the barracks library,' said Slabo. 'I told him to curtail the killing. He keeps hitting the wrong targets.'

* * *

They were standing outside the house Sabel was staying at. The street was poorly lit, although they were constructing street lights nearby. Niko had just been kissed.

'I have to go in now,' said Sabel without moving.

Niko licked his lips, not only did Sabel look like a trifle, she tasted like one too. She watched his tongue licking his lips.

'It's my lip-salve,' she said. 'Raspberry flavour.'

'Yeah, I think so,' said Niko. 'Well, good night then.'

'Goodnight.'

Nothing happened.

Sabel turned and began the slow process of unlocking the front door.

*　*　*

Clara was working the evening shift. The cinema goers, clubbers, drinkers, drifters and talkers thronging on and off her bus marvelled at her attire. Instead of the bus company uniform she wore her boots and her coat. Instead of tying her hair back with an elastic band she copied the hooker's look. Her head was full of candy coloured birds.

*　*　*

Zebedee, who had not checked the notice board in the barracks library, had another pop at his target that night. Once again he missed.

*　*　*

Niko hurried through the dark streets back under the dual carriage way to the suburban street. The living room light was still on in Laura's house. After skulking around for a while he was drawn, as if by a magnet, to the front door. He pressed the button and the little tune played. Laura's mother answered the door.

'I thought it was you. She's not here,' she said, allowing Niko to step in.

*   *   *

'Janja,' said Steiner. 'Pleased to meet you again. It's Steiner,' said Steiner helpfully, 'we met here yesterday.'

Clara, who five minutes before had finished her shift smiled.

'I remember you. In fact, it's rather hard to forget you.'

'You look fantastic,' said Steiner, touching one of the candy coloured birds in Clara's hair.

It was true, Clara felt fantastic, it had taken her a little while to take control of her wilful clothes. Now they were more or less trained. She crossed her legs.

*   *   *

'I would like you to fuck me – quite hard,' said Clara.

She and Steiner had moved on. They were in his flat. She was wearing only her boots and sunglasses. Steiner had no clothes at all.

THURSDAY, OCTOBER 31ST

At seven o'clock the following morning Clara closed the door on Steiner's apartment. She began descending the stairs to the lobby where the cleaner was pushing a mop over the floor. The big front door was wide open and sound of traffic spilled into the lobby. A woman carrying a small bag from a baker's shop was making her way up the staircase from the lobby. They met between floors.

'Hi,' said Clara.

Janja looked at Clara, the coat, the boots, the ridiculous hair, the sunglasses. Clara's expression changed. She noticed a flicker of disapproval in Janja's eyes.

'Are you going to see Steiner?' she asked.

Janja nodded.

Clara smiled.

'I suppose this is one of the pitfalls of sleeping with strangers,' said Janja.

'Speak for yourself,' said Clara. 'If he has any energy left, I'd quite like to watch.'

Janja drew her lips across her teeth.

'My God, are you his wife?' said Clara. 'Honestly, I had no idea – he never said anything.'

'No I'm not his wife.'

'His girlfriend?'

'No.'

'Oh,' said Clara. 'Goodbye.'

Janja watched as the woman hurried down into entrance hall and out through the front door.

Janja paused outside Steiner's door. She'd thought breakfast would be a good idea, a gift of some fresh croissants. She wasn't so sure now. After a moment or two she knocked. Steiner opened the door.

'Clara,' he said, 'what a pleasant surprise.'

He invited Janja in. They ate croissants, drank coffee and then went out.

*   *   *

Jani awoke that morning believing the window to be open. Only after a few minutes of blinking did he surmise that not only was the window open, the wall was open too. In fact, as he rolled his eyes around, he became aware of the fact that there were no walls or windows to speak of. A revision of the evidence around him seemed to suggest that he had spent the night outside. His bed was grass, the river gurgled past nearby and the steady hum of traffic rumbled in his ears. He was cold and covered in dew. Clearly he was outside, as a geographer he knew that. But there was one piece of evidence which confused him. He was sleeping with someone, who he originally assumed to be his wife. The stubbly texture of his partner's chin exploded that myth. Slowly Jani withdrew his arm from the neighbouring person. He sat up. With his head upright he seemed to be able to think straighter. He had a hangover, he could just about remember being in the old bar with Smoke, Priest and Wisdom. But there wasn't much else to go on. He surmised that somehow he must have staggered out of the bar and collapsed on the riverbank. The person who had assumed to be his wife was a actually a big burly man, a road sweeper perhaps, wearing a city council, luminous yellow plastic gilet, overalls and huge steel toe capped boots. He must also have staggered out of a different bar and collapsed on the riverbank. The fact that that they'd both gravitated to the same spot was not, according to the models used by human geographers to explain the flows of pedestrians and the shapes of towns, impossible. This was a spot where drunk people collapsed. A collapsing point.

Jani shook his head, he vowed never to drink again. Perhaps he bumped into the drunk council worker and the two of them had fallen to the ground in a wine fuelled embrace. But then he saw the man's face. The man's eyes stared wide open at the grass, trickles of dried blood running from the nose, mouth and ears. He was dead. Jani jerked back, horrified, pushing himself to his feet.

'Jesus,' he hissed, looking around distancing himself further.

Jani rubbed his eyes. Instinctively he moved away from the corpse. With every step backwards he felt a little better. He felt more like a passing pedestrian and less like a ... Jani sank to his knees. Technically speaking he had just slept with a dead man.

In an instant Jani knew what to do. He ran to the college, showered at the gymnasium and changed into the spare clothes he kept in his locker. Then, with his first class, he led an expedition to the riverbank to gather geographical data. Jani patrolled the periphery as he watched his young geographers fan out across the area, clip-boards and tape measures in hand, intent on recording the distances between willow trees. It took a little while for them discover the corpse. Some of the students were deliberately ignoring it, presumably, not wishing to be troubled with the business of accounting for a dead council worker in their data. The more gifted and talented students must have realised that the discovery of the council worker might invalidate the day's measurements. One of Jani's less able students discovered the body. He shouted, they gathered, then they called the police. There were police-men, cars, more measurements, a smartly dressed inspector took statements from the student who came across the body. Others took a statement from Jani. Jani said how surprised he was.

As he and his students trooped back to the college discussing the murder on the riverbank, Jani could think of only one thing. Now, he needed a drink.

* * *

When the Dormouse Master watched the sunrise illuminate his name, as if scribbled onto the forest by the finger of God, he knew he was right. There, on the side of the valley in front of him, for all to see, in thirty foot letters cut into the pine trees was the ultimate in crop circle art, the words 'Dormouse Master' stretched for almost a kilometre, etched into the green cloak of the forested valley. People would come from miles around to see his title just as they went to Hollywood to see the sign on the hill there. His unique trade mark in his unique forest, pulled from the ground with his bare hands, would go down in history. There would be no question of preserving the name for the good of all businesspeople. His trade mark was his name, he had given it to himself, he had scratched it in the land and now he would make it legal. He gazed at his handiwork – it was a landmark with such a lot of distinctive character that it could no longer be regarded as merely a name – it was a work of art.

After the triumphant dawn, the Dormouse Master left the forest and returned to the town, where he delivered his yellow form, requesting an appeal against Mr Frayling's decision at the High Court.

The Dormouse Master spent the rest of the day in the city library, reading about the law of trade marks.

* * *

Niko was up to his elbows again. Mashed pumpkins were easier to deal with than people, geography essays, dead bodies on the river bank and women. The old man needed as much pumpkin as possible. And although his cooking skills were basic, notwithstanding the fact that he made a lot of mess which pissed his mother off, Niko found that he actually liked boiling up pumpkins, pouring the soup into little pickle jars, cataloguing it and freezing it. It made him feel as if he was doing something useful. Everything else was pandemonium.

There was a buzz from the front door. Niko answered.

'Hello.'

'Niko, it's me,' said the voice. 'I'm back.'

'Laura!' cried Niko. 'Where the hell have you been?'

'I just needed a few days on my own,' said Laura. 'Can I come in.'

'I'm doing soup,' said Niko. 'No.'

'Please,' said Laura.

'Can't you come back another time?' asked Niko.

'I've missed you, I can explain,' said Laura.

'Can you?' said Niko.

'Stop messing around,' said Laura. 'Let me in.'

Niko pressed the button and unlocked the door. Then he opened the apartment door and listened, he could hear Laura's feet tapping on the stairs, the lift was broken.

* * *

Jani sighed. He sipped his beer as he held his audience rapt. He was telling them the latest instalment of his story. The day had been extraordinary. But the events it contained were born in the middle of the night. A time he couldn't remember.

'How drunk was I when I left this bar?' he asked.

'You could walk,' said Priest.

'Just,' said Smoke.

'We watched you fall over,' said Wisdom. 'But you got up, so we thought you were OK.'

'I can't remember anything, but one of my students, Laura, told me.'

'Is she the bit on the side?' asked Smoke.

'I hardly think that's an appropriate expression,' said Jani.

'Well is she?' asked Smoke.

'She was the student who has been sexually harassing me and plaguing my life – if that's what you mean, yes she is.'

'Did you give her her marching orders; did you finish with her?'

'Yes I did. Well, she finished with me, actually. But I hardly think that the term 'finish' does the conversation justice.'

'Shame on you,' said Priest, producing a cigar from his pocket and running it beneath his nose.

She told me she followed me from this bar,' said Jani.

'I told you she was a stalker,' said Priest.

'She tried to tie me to a tree,' said Jani. 'She wanted to make love to me, she was obsessed with me.'

'Oh dear,' said Smoke.

'But I was too drunk, I couldn't stand up.'

'Brewer's droop,' noted Wisdom.

Jani ignored the ridiculous statement.

'We were disturbed, attacked, in a way,' said Jani.

'The Dragon Bridge Killer?' gasped Smoke. 'You're lucky to be alive. Everybody's talking about him. A serial killer who lives under the bridge.'

He rolled his eyes.

'No,' said Jani. 'Just a nutter with a knife asking for money, we gave him some change. I'm starting to get to know him quite well. Then Laura ran off. She said that she'd had enough.'

'Of what?' asked Wisdom.

The Priest interrupted:

'Seeing the poor man with a knife probably brought things home to her,' said Priest. 'She probably realised that what she was doing wasn't a game. It just took the intervention of a third party, someone to stumble upon the pair of you, caught in a ridiculous situation to bring home the absurd nature of her obsessive behaviour.'

Jani nodded.

'You know,' he said, 'that's pretty much what she said to me today. When she told me what we said last night. Although, she did mention one other thing.'

'What?' they all asked.

'I'm sorry,' said Jani, clasping his head in his hands. He closed his eyes and sucked in air through his nose.

'But you're her teacher,' said the Priest. 'You're to blame.'

Jani nodded.

'It's a fucking mess.'

'We all make mistakes,' said Priest.

'I slept with a dead man,' whined Jani.

'You were drunk, probably a bit emotional after being dumped by your seventeen year old student, a lot of people would have done the same thing,' said Priest.

There was a pause as they all considered whether this was really true or not.

'She came to college today for the first time for weeks. She told me again. 'It's over', she said.'

Jani sipped his lager.

'She didn't want me anymore,' he added.

'Thank god for that, she could have killed you,' said Smoke.

'It's a big relief,' said Jani.

Wisdom stood up and walked to the gaming machine.

'In my opinion,' he stated, 'it's the least of your problems – you have no recollection of what happened to you after she left. All you know is that you woke up cuddling a dead man. If the police ever find that out – they'll stitch you up. You'll go down for murder.'

'I didn't do it,' said Jani. 'It's obvious. I was drunk, tired, I just fell asleep on the river bank. Someone must have shot the man. He must have staggered to where I was sleeping and died next to me.'

The Priest stroked his beard.

'The cops don't care so much about what happened, they're more interested in statistics. You need a better alibi.'

'But I can't remember anything, I was blind drunk,' said Jani. 'I've got to stop all this damn drinking.'

'You should stay in here with us. Trouble only visits us in here,' said Smoke, 'Trouble never stays – we're far too jolly for Trouble.'

'Do you think I should just confess to the cops?'

'No!' said the three men in unison.

'I'll lie low, keep out of the way, try to make things up with my wife,' said Jani.

'Don't tell her,' said Priest.

'Don't tell her what?'

'Don't tell her anything,' said Priest.

Vala drove, Slabo pulled the glove box open. A road atlas of Europe fell out. He opened it and surveyed the emptiness of the North Norwegian coast.

'There's only one road in the North of Norway,' he said, 'let's go there.'

'We're not running,' said Vala, leaning on the horn as the car screamed in front of a bus ponderously negotiating a left turn.

As she drove away she unwound the window and gestured at the driver. The bus trumpeted its horn like an angry elephant.

'Slabo,' said Vala, 'you can forget any ideas of running away. We're going to sort this out. It's not too late. This is like dealing with an infection – everybody's gone nuts.'

'Zebedee's crazy,' said Slabo. 'That's two nut-case psychopaths I've put on the streets. I'm supposed to be 'lighting the night'.'

'You're the Minster for Culture,' said Vala. 'You have no business getting involved with street lights and crime anyway.'

Slabo hung his head, he turned the page and looked at Finland.

'What about Finland?'

'It's too dark in the winter. You'd finish up drinking lighter fuel, sniffing glue and marrying an elk.'

'Sounds OK,' said Slabo. 'When you think of the alternative.'

'Which is what?'

'A fucking media trial. When you look at the facts, a good brief could make me look like a war criminal. I've killed four people.'

'You haven't,' said Vala. 'That's exactly my point. You just think you have. You just have to think you haven't and history will prove you right.'

They turned left into the Black Forest, driving past old tenement blocks, warehouses, the Tivoli hotel, looking over a park in which huge monkey puzzle trees scrammed the sky. Behind the trees was the vast car park, the old parade ground; after that, the barracks.

Vala pulled up, she stepped out of the car purposefully. Slabo, lugubrious, replaced the atlas in the glove-box before joining Vala and guiding her through the huge metal door, across the stair-less lobby, along the musty corridor and into the library full of rotting books on tactics.

They stood in front of the green baize notice board. Vala removed Slabo's order commanding Zebedee to abort the mission. Then she read the other messages. Pinned to the board on the backs of bus tickets were the communiques from Zebedee.

'Mission 4.21: operation Falcon's Beak. Activation date: Oct 13th.'

'Have successfully completed weapons testing.'

'Have killed the murderer.'

'Mistook murderer for fisherman. Have killed fisherman.'

'Have conducted analysis of the riverside.'

'Have completed the mission.'

'Have killed another fisherman.'

'Have re-assessed the subject's camouflage abilities.'

'Have increased level of awareness from 7 to 9.9.'

'Have killed the subject.'

'Have killed a council worker.'

'Have increased logistical input.'

After reading each note Vala un-picked the drawing pin attaching it to the baize.

Slabo wrote a fresh note.

'What are you doing?' hissed Vala.

Slabo held up a piece of paper with the word 'stop' written on it.

'No more notes,' she said, tearing the paper from Slabo's hand. 'We have to find him. We'll go to the riverside.'

'But the place is crawling with cops,' said Slabo.

'If Drago's still alive, he'll be hanging out down there, so that's where Zebedee will be. He's nothing if not persistent.'

*　　*　　*

After passing the morning with Steiner, Janja had gone to work. She'd organised the labs, set up meetings with colleagues and e-mailed several students about their work. On the way home she stopped at the shop. Karen greeted her like an old friend.

'The police came back,' she said, as Janja paid for her evening paper.

'They think there's a serial killer on the loose, they think it's him.'

'Who?' asked Janja.

'My robber,' said Karen, with something bordering on pride in her voice. 'The Troll Man who lives under the bridge. He's killed two people, he's robbed loads more.'

'Hmmm,' said Janja, 'your guy had a kitchen knife, this one has a gun.'

'Yes but that doesn't mean that my robber couldn't get a gun from somewhere,' said Karen. 'The police think he did it. They've got patrols all over the river bank. In the night there's an officer stationed just outside my shop, in case he comes back. They're convinced its him.'

Janja wasn't convinced. She felt a twinge, a slight stirring, a familiar voice within. It was like detecting an old friend in a strange railway carriage and then finding that they are not there.

'Your robber has nothing to do with the real story,' said Janja, her eyes glinting as she looked behind Karen's shoulder.

'The Dragon Bridge has a road block on it,' said Karen.

'I know,' said Janja. 'It's pointless. The police have no idea.'

Karen folded her arms.

'What makes you so sure?' asked Karen.

Janja thought for moment, then she spoke apologetically.

'I'm sorry, I guess I'm just a bit tetchy. It's good that they're trying to do something.'

Janja walked the short distance home, noticing the large number of police vehicles parked in the side streets.

When she arrived in her flat, she began brewing a coffee. She couldn't settle down to her marking. In the end she decided to take a walk. Perhaps that's what she told herself – in fact she was looking for someone.

*   *   *

Clara had spent the day with her son. She'd picked him up from her mother's apartment, but there had been no school because he had a bad cold. Her mother also reported the possibility that he had eggs in his hair. Clara spent a reasonably productive morning combing them out with a nit comb. In the afternoon she pushed him around the local park in his buggy. He didn't want to get up and play. He just dozed under his blanket.

At six o'clock his father appeared, on time for once. Clara packed the boy off with a little overnight bag and strict instructions to keep him warm and well combed. She went home, put on her coat and boots, her stunning make up and candy-floss hair. There was something about dressing like the hooker that made her feel as if she was on holiday. She had no intention of becoming a hooker, but the fact that simply changing her clothes had such a dramatic effect on how people related to her made her feel as different as she used to every time she stepped off an aeroplane. It was like being able to take a city break at will. In her bus driver's sweater she was completely anonymous. She liked that. In her hooker's coat she was the focus of attention; she liked that too. More than that, things happened to her. She'd met Steiner for one. Who else might she meet? A new life in the coat was opening up.

Clara didn't feel like revisiting the pick-up bar. Steiner clearly had enough on his plate and she couldn't be bothered to listen to his explanations for the woman she'd met outside his flat. She left her apartment without much idea of where she would end up. She drifted through the deepening dusk and, in time, realised where she was going. It would be interesting to find out what it felt like in the Tivoli Hotel. What it felt like to be her – the owner of the coat.

* * *

The Dormouse Master was also walking. He'd joined the library (with difficulty – because his address, which was more of a grid reference than a postal code – was barely comprehensible to the librarians). He'd persuaded them to accept his membership application, by asking them to ring Mr Frayling at the Office Of Industrial Property and explaining that he was engaged in legal research. In the end Mr Frayling had very kindly agreed to act as a kind of guarantor. Any fines incurred by the Dormouse Master, who for administrative purposes was given the name Mr Master for his library ticket, would be sent to Mr Frayling's office address. He would then pay them and recoup the losses from the Dormouse Master by visiting his hut in the forest.

Now, as dusk fell, the Dormouse Master descended the marble steps that flowed from the great revolving doors of the city's library, carrying an arm-full of legal text books. He felt like a student, indeed, there were plenty of them around, popping in and out of the library with their computer bags slung over their shoulders, texting each other on their phones and talking noisily about, as far as Mr Master could make out, complex matters.

He liked the feeling the library gave him. He looked forward to taking new books home. He wanted to travel through their words in just the same way as he conducted himself in the forest. He didn't really want to understand it all: he just liked being in there, where the letters were like leaves and sentences seemed like branches. The Dormouse Master enjoyed being around the students too and he loved becoming a member of the library. He relished the new knowledge he was acquiring about the law of trade marks. For the first time in his life he felt that he had a place to be in the town and something to do in it. He didn't feel the need to retreat to his hunting lodge, he felt pleasure at being drawn from his shell: he felt wonder at the fact that nobody seemed to mind him being there, silent, with other silent people in a vast wooden room full of paper.

The Dormouse Master walked down the hill that leads from the library, past the open-air theatre with its busy student cafes and bars, to the river. After following the road a little way, the river bank opened out and there were benches where he could sit, and, by angling his books in such a way as to catch the last rays of sunset spilling onto the Dragon Bridge, he could read.

Nearby a police-man stood guard over a patch of ground, cordoned off with blue and red tape.

A bearded tourist, wearing sandals, white socks, long baggy shorts and a T-shirt promoting the delights of Lake Chiemsee in Bavaria sat down next to the Dormouse Master. He opened a large camera bag and began to set up tripod, fiddling with his light meters and lenses, focussing on the bridge which was glowing with the orange light of a reflected sunset.

The Dormouse Master paid no attention to the photographer.

*   *   *

Janja had also decided to walk through the reds and browns of the evening; to drink a coffee by the low white marble columns at the market and meander along the banks of the river where the willow trees touch the slow-moving, almost still, surface. She passed a couple, a boy and a girl, or perhaps a young man and a young woman, holding hands, deep in conversation. She felt almost compelled to ask them what they were talking about, they seemed so wrapped up in themselves, so serious. She watched them intently, rudely, but they didn't notice her, they swung off the main road and took a seat on the riverbank, near the Dragon Bridge.

As Janja strolled on, soothed by the calm water, gurgling relentlessly downwards through drains, down into the river and then down into the ground, she felt motivated, as if some invisible hand was pushing her forwards, nudging her towards the Dragon Bridge, as if there was something to be seen there.

'Gregor,' she muttered, 'do you really think that there is actually something going on in this town?'

'Yes,' came the answer.

Janja froze. She checked behind her, her eyes flicked around the street corners, the lamp posts and the tree trunks, anything behind which Gregor could be taking cover. She stared at the fat, bloodshot moon, low on the horizon. Tears filled her eyes as she recognised its familiar grin. She sighed with relief.

'Jesus, Gregor. I've missed you,' she whispered.

Her eyes widened, and a broad smile spread across her lips as she searched for the source of the sound.

*　*　*

Slabo and Vala had parked near the bridge. They'd just been talking to some of the police officers on the bridge. They'd introduced themselves, but the officers had already recognised Slabo. They patted his back saying that his 'light the night' campaign was exactly the kind of thing they needed. More light in the night would help them see what was going on, it also improved the images on CCTV cameras which were notoriously difficult to use in court when the light wasn't good.

They walked into a little bar near the bridge. From here it was possible to watch the river and not be seen. The bar was suitably anonymous and quite empty. A drunk man who looked like a college lecturer sat sleeping with his head on a round table next to a gambling machine. A fat man played the machine. A thin man smoked outside. A man with a big beard leant on the bar sipping a glass of beer, pausing only to sniff a large cigar.

They ordered coffees and took a window seat. The landlord had placed a pumpkin lantern in the window. The light flickered around their faces. From outside things looked warm and convivial. As usual, when they were in public places, Vala and Slabo spoke in whispers.

'He'll be disguised,' said Vala.

'I know,' said Slabo, watching a woman walking her dog walk past.

'But he won't strike yet, it's too busy, he'll be here, staking out his patch, all we have to do is apprehend him.'

* * *

After visiting the Tivoli Hotel, Clara walked towards town. She wasn't sure whether her visit to the Tivoli had been worth it. Perhaps she just wanted to show the original owner of the coat and boots what a silly mistake they'd made by taking to them to the market to sell. In any instance, the hotel had been a great disappointment. It was dull and she wasn't quite sure what she was doing there. The old man at the counter had shown no interest in her. He hadn't even responded to her 'good afternoon'. He just raised his eyebrows without moving his eyes from the small screen he'd concealed beneath the counter, next to the old maps. He hadn't even recognised her, or perhaps, she thought, as she strolled along the streets turning heads with her new look, he had.

* * *

In the culvert beneath the Dragon Bridge, something splashed. Cold fingers grappled with the heavy metal cover, prizing it from the drain it protected with a groan. A thin, hungry, desperate man with wild red eyes and squid skin crawled in. Drago slid into the drain, dragging the iron hatch shut behind him. He had been downriver, near the hotel where he had killed her, in the place by the water, where he spent most of days, recalling, with regret, how he strangled her in the mud, remembering the panic in her eyes as he crushed her neck.

He had seen her again. She had come back to life. Drago's screams echoed through the guts of the city, but above ground, its ears heard nothing. The ghost of the woman he had murdered had returned to haunt him.

Drago rested his back on the concave wall of the drain. Could he kill her again? If he'd done it once, wouldn't that make him better at it a second time? Was it possible to kill a dead person? Drago pushed at the hatch and slipped out. Slowly he slithered upstream, sliding low through the grass until he reached the safety of a willow tree. The cops were everywhere. He had to do it now and move on, it was only a matter of time before they started to search the sewers.

* * *

Janja watched as the woman with the boots marched downtown. She wondered whether she was on her way to see Steiner. She'd asked him about her over coffee in the morning, but Steiner hadn't explained her presence in his flat very effectively. He'd said that he didn't really know who she was. To Janja this evasiveness was unremarkable, what intrigued her was the fact that she and the lady in the coat shared the same name.

'That's the one,' said Gregor.

Janja's pulse quickened. She followed the woman onto the

Dragon Bridge, hiding next to a man selling roasted chestnuts behind one of the big green dragons. After Clara had crossed, Janja hurried over, taking cover behind the dragon on the opposite side, where an accordion player was setting up her music stand and collapsible fishing stool.

*　*　*

Clara paraded down from the bridge feeling like a movie star. Perhaps it was the fact that she was now almost in the centre of town, perhaps she was simply growing more accustomed to her outlandish appearance. She felt as if she was the subject of everyone's gaze. She was a walking work of art.

Slabo spotted her.

'It's her,' hissed Slabo. 'She's back.'

Vala had stopped listening to Slabo.

'A ghost,' wheezed Slabo.

'Hmmm,' said Vala, ignoring him.

Slabo stared through the glass up the road towards the Dragon Bridge. On one side were parked cars and a row of neat little shops and offices, on the other, turf leading down to the willow trees and the river bank, a few benches, students reading in the last rays of afternoon light, a photographer setting up for some shots of the magic hour. Walking straight towards him was Barbie, the woman he'd mistakenly removed. For an instant Slabo sighed with relief. The whole thing had been a terrible dream – the girl was still alive. There was no need to worry about anything.

Slabo hesitated before spreading the good news to Vala. He watched Vala, also peering through the window. Somehow he didn't think she'd appreciate his new discovery. He watched the woman again – perhaps she was a little bigger than Barbie, although she was certainly wearing her clothes. It was Slabo who had bought her the new coat and boots. Vala paid no attention to Slabo. She scanned the scene with a less frantic eye. She wanted to be the first to spot Zebedee.

*   *   *

Dusk was falling, and it was too dark for the Dormouse Master to read properly. He folded his books and shambled off towards the bridge. The tourist had set up his equipment maybe ten meters away. He watched the Dormouse Master amble towards the road and he stroked his long red beard. Then something caught his eye. It wasn't much, the merest flicker of a shadow, like a jay clattering through a hawthorn hedge. Zebedee saw Drago leaping from his cover behind a willow tree. He spun around and reached into his camera bag.

*   *   *

Clara had left the bridge and was making her way along the road next to the river bank. The accordion player, sitting on an old collapsible fishing stool at the base of one of the fat dragon plinths, began to play a baleful old waltz. Clara enjoyed the sound of her boots on the pavement, they clicked in time with the music, accentuating the sway of her hips. She was only aware for the tiniest instant of a shadowy shape in the far-flung fringe of her peripheral vision. A man rushed up at her. He launched himself at her, trying to push her to the ground. Janja, twenty meters behind quickened her pace. She'd seen a little more. A man, dripping wet, clutching a knife, panting like a dog, had launched himself from a hiding place behind a tree. Janja ran to help Clara. She grabbed the man by his slimy shoulders and pulled, trying to keep the knife away from Clara.

'It's him,' hissed Vala pointing at the disturbance.

Slabo covered his eyes. He couldn't watch – the vision walking down the road was like a zombie. The re-energised perambulating body of his former lover. That was her coat, her boots. He hadn't slept enough, he knew that, but this time he wasn't seeing things. He shrunk back from the window in horror, pulling and pinching his skin, trying to wake himself up.

'She's alive,' he whispered.

The Dormouse Master turned as he reached the roadside. As he did, his foot landed on a piece of plastic tape left by the police. He slipped.

Clara let out a scream.

The police on the bridge didn't hear. They were too close to the accordion player. But the one guarding the scene of the earlier crime on the riverbank did hear the cry, although he couldn't tell from where it came.

Aiming carefully through his telescopic sight at the Troll Man, Zebedee squeezed the trigger.

His bullet flew straight at the assailant from his position by the tripod next to the river. Satisfied that this time he had struck bull's-eye, Zebedee shoved his specially crafted weapon into the case for long photographic lenses. He began packing up the rest of his equipment, unaware of the calamity that was unfolding.

His bullet was well directed. But the Dormouse Master, still thinking about words, the law of trade marks, his new library books, the lovely long desks in the old reading room had stumbled and, almost as if guided by some devilish hand, dropped into the trajectory of the projectile. The bullet struck the Dormouse Master in the head, smashing his brain and silencing him before he could even think to cry out. Like a chicken with no head, his legs moved him on;

he tottered, unheard and unseen down the river bank, his hands, gripping his books and pulling them to his chest in a reflex reaction.

Vala and Slabo watched from behind the pumpkin in the Banana bar and the other drinkers joined them, their eyes flickering around the tableaux in front of them, as if they were trying to understand a great painting in the city's art gallery.

As the Dormouse Master took his final automatic steps, Janja struggled with the Troll Man, knocking the knife out his hand. She screamed at the police officer for help. This time he heard. He drew a gun, fired in the air and rushed over. Now the cops on the bridge knew something was up. The whole river bank seemed to erupt with activity.

But nobody saw the Dormouse Master fall and slip into the river. The river removed the Dormouse Master with a greedy gurgle and he was drawn downwards and away forever.

'Damn,' muttered Zebedee under his breath when, finally, he reached a safe enough distance to turn to review his handiwork.

Clara and Janja had the upper hand over the assailant before the strong arm of the law arrived. Janja had smashed his knife hand against a wall and he'd lost his grip. Without the blade he was weak. He coughed, he burbled nonsense about someone called Barbie whom he had killed. He screamed at Clara for being a ghost. He grabbed the coat Clara was wearing, clutching it in his fists.

'I killed you! I killed you!' he cried.

Janja thought that Troll Man seemed to be talking to the coat rather than Clara. Clara shrank away from him. Janja thought Clara seemed to be trying to wriggle out of the coat – almost as if it had nothing to do with her.

Two police-men rushed down from the bridge. They pulled spindly young Troll Man away.

Clara wilted, scared out of her wits. She fell to the floor, her leather legs sticking out from under her coat like drain pipes. What was she doing? Who did she think she was? She should have been at home with her boy. Or, possibly, driving her bus. She sobbed and remonstrated with herself staining her face with streams of make-up splodges.

Janja tried to calm Clara down. But Clara was hysterical. She screamed at Janja, the woman whose boyfriend she'd been screwing. Why the fuck was she following her?

Janja tried to say that she was just out for a walk. But it sounded lame. And although she felt it was true, we all know, when we are walking, we are always being pushed or pulled in one direction or someone or other. The truth of the matter was that Janja was following Clara, she just didn't understand why, or perhaps it's more accurate to say, she didn't think that anybody would have believed her if she'd told them why.

Jani, still sleeping on his table, saw nothing. The others in the café, crowded at the window scrutinised the action. Vala made calculations. Slabo held his head in his hands muttering the name Drago over and again: Drago – the idiot. The Priest and Smoke kept everyone informed.

'Look,' said Priest, 'now they're going to take the monster away.'

The police cuffed the attacker.

'The man is a monster – he looks more like a fish,' said Smoke.

Janja stared at the knife on the ground.

Clara tried to compose herself.

'It's OK,' said Janja. 'He's just some junkie. That knife, he stole it from a restaurant. He was just after your money. He didn't kill you. You're going to be OK.'

Clara nodded. That much was true. In fact, she realised, although she was shocked, inappropriately dressed and, to be honest, rather embarrassed, no serious damage had been done. Perhaps she'd learned a lesson. Although what that could be wasn't clear at the moment.

Clara glanced at her assailant: his skin was yellowy white, like the underside of carp, his hair was matted and streams of mud ran like blood around his bony cheeks. His blue eyes appeared to have been electrified, his mouth was open, his teeth were chipped, his clothes, half eaten away, clung to his bony ribs and knees. He was trying to speak. Clara seemed to terrify him, but she had no idea why. He pulled at her coat.

'What's the matter?' she stammered.

Before the Troll Man could find a word, another police officer smashed his face with butt of his gun.

The spectators in the café drew their breath, shocked by the unnecessary brutality. Sirens began to wail as police cars arrived, an ambulance, even the fire brigade. They took Clara to hospital leaving Janja at the scene, providing details and witness statements to the police and then the journalists. She watched as the inspector with the Italian suit and the silver tie pin, marched over the bridge. He issued orders to a young colleague about the positioning of tape and the traffic flow on the bridge. When he'd finished, the inspector hurried on. He spat into the river and walked briskly down to the crime scene, where several of his men had gathered.

'They got their man,' announced Priest turning to the bar.

'I'll make sure of that,' said Vala.

Priest brought everybody glasses of brandy. They drank to soothe their nerves. Vala couldn't help feel it was a little like a toast – but to what? Crime prevention? Murder? Smashing people's faces? Nobody spoke as they raised their glasses and drank. Then, as if reconstituted by that little alcoholic buzz, Vala set to work. She could see a way out. But they had to move quickly.

She took Slabo by the arm and led him out of the bar. Priest, Smoke and the others said goodbye, they commented that it was still early in the evening, who knew what additional catastrophes were going to occur outside later on. Vala said that she'd had quite enough excitement for one day.

Jani stirred slightly but he didn't wake.

* * *

Vala drove. Slabo was in shock. Although he'd taken his hands away from his face, he kept going on about Barbie, the dead one who'd mysteriously come back to life. Vala didn't believe this for a second. She reminded him that they were watching events in half-light through a grimy café window with their lines of sight half-obscured by willow trees. The girl Slabo had seen was merely extremely reminiscent of someone he remembered.

They sped to the barracks first, screeching to a halt and rushing into the grim old lobby. At night, with only thin beams of leaked light squeezing in through the gaps in the collapsing blinds and the sound of rats, cats and hidden people stirring on rotting boards, the place felt like the departure lounge for Hades. At least that's what Slabo said to Vala as he fought back his fear and shouted out for Zebedee.

He arrived, through the front door, carrying his cameras and guns in his bags, with his tourist books still under his arm.

Slabo grabbed him.

'You've got to stop,' he yelled.

Zebedee pulled his red beard away from his chin. He nodded.

'I've never had a job like this – the fellow you're after is good, very good. I think he's professional,' he said.

'We don't care, Zebedee,' said Vala. 'We just want you to stop shooting people. We'll pay you the rest of the money - just stop.'

'Can't think who it could be though: the Baedekers are in Hamburg and I know Ziff's busy with something-or-other in Graz... Could be someone new, but to be honest, they're too good to be fresh starters.'

Zebedee rubbed the sides of his cheeks, clearing away remnants of glue.

'Just stop,' said Slabo, handing a brown paper envelope to Zebedee. Zebedee felt it in his hand, it was approximately the right weight.

FRIDAY, NOVEMBER 1ST

That night Slabo and Vala stayed in a hotel. They chose the Tivoli for the same reason as everyone else does – they didn't want to be noticed. They didn't even want to notice each other. They made love in their room, which still contained a photocopier and, over breakfast, in an anonymous basement, filled with aluminium legged tables covered with purple paper table cloths, they enjoyed orange squash, instant coffee and yesterday's bread with plastic blisters of strawberry jam. It was the best breakfast, the best hotel, either of them could remember.

When they emerged into the lobby, Slabo leant casually on an old mermaid as Vala checked her messages. The news from The Department was good. The Troll Man from under the bridge had died in custody, whilst he was asleep.

* * *

Karen grinned at Janja as she waited for her change.

'Everything all right?' she asked.

'No,' said Janja. 'I was just recalling something a friend said to me. Do you ever get that thing when you can hear their voices in your head?'

Karen stared at her till.

'You mean like a loony?' asked Karen. 'Of course not. I've had it with nutters in this shop. The last one I had tried to kill me.'

'Don't worry, I'm talking about something far more prosaic. You know, when you hear a funny line on the TV and remember it the next day, or you remember something someone said in a lecture, or even something you said.'

Karen shook her head.

'I remember stuff,' she said. 'But only when I want to. I don't like it when stuff keeps coming at me, whether I wanted it to or not.'

Janja took her newspaper. The headline was simple: 'Troll Man Dies'.

'Thank goodness for some good news,' said Karen as Janja walked out of the shop and towards the university.

Janja worked as productively as possible all day. But she kept looking for Gregor. In store cupboards, in the reprographics room, hiding in the cloak rooms. She wanted him back. She needed to talk to him because something was worrying her – what if he'd been wrong?

In the evening, as she loitered near the Dragon Bridge, keeping an eye on the young couple canoodling on a bench by a willow tree below overlooking the river (she was sure they were the same as the ones who had been there the night before. How odd, why would anyone knowingly canoodle on a crime scene?), Janja had begun to doubt whether Gregor's certainty that a plot could not be discovered in this city was right. She wanted to find Gregor, to ask him whether she'd discovered a plot that was worth investigating or not and to ask him for his advice as to how to go about solving it. But, notwithstanding the fact that she spoke to him out loud, from the middle of the bridge, all that she could hear was the same sad song. The accordion player had taken up her position near the dragon, she kept repeating the old limping waltz.

'Gregor,' shouted Janja, as she stormed off the bridge. 'Why are you never around when I need you?'

She looked at the moon. It was higher, brighter and smaller than before – he wasn't there.

* * *

Over a glass of beer, in the tiny bar with a big bay window overlooking the bridge, with a drunk and some loquacious time-wasters close at hand, Janja began to feel even more uneasy - as if the pretty scene she was observing, with its fat dragon-topped bridge and smooth-sided arch, languid water, drooping willow trees and little puffs of chestnut smoke had been deliberately constructed by some clever designer, intent on obscuring something terrible, by drawing the eye upwards towards the castle-topped hillside and the early evening stars, obligingly pointing out the purple sky.

It wasn't as if she didn't know what had happened. She'd witnessed an attack; she'd watched the Dragon Bridge killer brought to justice; she'd seen the man who stole the contents of Karen's till cornered and captured. She'd been telling herself the same thing all day - it was just another sad little, inconsequential Gregorian story about a junkie who stole a knife and robbed a shop. He'd told her what would happen – and it had.

But Janja couldn't take her eyes off the bridge. She'd heard the sound of a man's face collapsing and now she knew, because she'd read her paper, that the character from beneath the bridge, who she had fought with, died in custody soon afterwards 'in his sleep'.

It was something to do with the river. Janja watched it, ignoring the sound of the ludicrous conversation in the background. In the end the river would flow past any obstacle. Janja stared out at the water, quietly slipping through the picture, disappearing beneath the fat dragons, cooling themselves in the October half-light.

'Does it bring it in, or suck it out?'

Janja turned to see who was responsible for the question. It wasn't who she'd hoped for. One of the men, the one with a beard, was standing by her table also looking through the window. Gregor was nowhere to be seen. Janja turned back to the window.

'Trouble, I mean,' said Priest, still staring through the glass. 'Does the river...'

'I know what you mean,' interrupted Janja. 'Now get lost.'

She scrutinized the scene, hunting for a sign. The picture was as pretty as the top of a dusty jigsaw box, the kind that gets stacked up in ramshackle piles in the store rooms of old libraries.

Her attention was drawn back, again, to the river. She stared more intently, almost as though she knew that there was something to see, in spite of its absence. That, if permitted, it would emerge, pulled out by the force of her gaze. She felt as if she was in her laboratory, before things went wrong, working her bench in college. What she could see, she realised, was an experiment. Somewhere in the scene there was a piece of datum that would bring order to the mix up and that would give her a nudge towards a working hypothesis. All Gregor did was grumble about the fact that, as far as he could see, there wasn't anything worth investigating because folks weren't interesting enough to merit the effort. Now Janja disagreed. Gregor had missed the point. Something was going on but, like dark matter, or gravity waves, it wasn't readily apparent. The indications were that nothing made sense, or perhaps, that nothing made sense without the missing piece. The job of a scientist, muttered Janja, is not to give up.

Janja thought about the previous night and, with the aid of a pencil and serviette, she began to sketch the scene on the little round marble-topped table in front of her. She put in the bridge, the willows, the passing cars, the streetlight, the police roadblock, a few buildings - to give scale, some musical notes - to remind her of the accordion tune; and the high turrets of the castle in the background to give depth, even some chestnut smoke - to suggest mystery. She added the girl in the coat, two lovers kissing on the opposite bank, some tourist taking photographs, the cop in the Italian coat, the uniformed men with their long streamers of stripy tape, the slithering assailant who got his face bashed in; she drew herself, standing near the bridge, just about to run and help the woman in the leather coat. She even drew the bar she was in, with the spectators peering out through her window. Almost as an afterthought, as if she were trying to bring a little sense of fluidity to the blank space between two lines where the river ran, she drew a swirl in the water. It made the picture look better, it put the water in motion.

It was nothing, a little pencil mark, about five millimetres long, barely perceptible on the surface of the serviette. Janja drew her breath when she saw it.

She'd heard something besides music, police sirens, screams, thumps and threats. Her ears had picked up a noise which, until she looked at the surface of the water, or her interpretation of the surface of the water as represented on her serviette with a tiny squiggle, her eyes had overlooked. She giggled, she almost spoke to herself, but she held back – she didn't want to encourage the conversationalists: what a bad student – making assumptions, leaping to uninteresting conclusions, assuming that critical voices were right, following the herd and ignoring the evidence in front of her own eyes and ears.

It was the sound. The sound of a splosh.

Janja emphasised the splosh sound on her map of the river.

What, she wondered, had made that noise? Did she recall a moan, prior to the splosh?

Yes.

Who had made the moan?

Someone else had been present at the demise of the Troll Man. All that was left of the missing individual was an apparently insignificant sploshing sound lodged somewhere in Janja's somewhat unpredictable imagination. Now, she began to sketch him onto her serviette; he occupied a surprisingly large space right at the centre of her image. The more she thought about the man with the books, the more details she remembered. Who was the tumbling man in the middle, who nobody had seen, who disappeared into the river?

It is said that, many years ago, there lived a man who could remember exactly what it was like to be born. He recalled being forced out of his mother's body, he remembered being cut adrift and the first sensation of air on the surface of his lungs, what it felt like to fit into the palm of someone else's hand, how extraordinary it is to open your eyes for the first time and see the light. Perhaps Janja felt like this. Scientists are notoriously bad at describing their eureka moments, the moments when everything changes, their descriptions are full of flashes, curtains opening, dawns, sunrises and other pyrotechnic effects. In truth, at this moment, Janja felt a sensation which could not be described in a positive way. It might best be summarised as a wave of nausea or frustration or anger or rage or perhaps even something more powerful than that. If Priest had interrupted Janja at this moment, she would have smashed her fist into his face, because she could tell by the way the Dormouse Master looked in her drawing that he was nothing like Gregor.

A tear dropped from the tip of Janja's nose, twinkling and turning in the air. It soaked into the serviette. Janja looked at the Dormouse Master, she touched his face with her finger. She drew more details. She smiled as she noticed his books and tried to read the titles.

'Hmm,' she whispered, 'I don't blame you for hiding them. You don't want to broadcast your interests. It's a bit cheap.'

There was something about talking to the man. The invisible, non-existent man. The one who she'd just drawn. The one who she knew was real. Somehow it brought everything out. It was too much. Janja began to cry. She didn't know why. The man on the serviette, she understood, was different. She touched his face again.

'A plot is what an investigation requires,' she muttered through gritted teeth and tears. Unwilling to use her serviette, but anxious not to draw attention to herself, she pushed her forearm over her eyes, trying to make the gesture seem normal. Or, at least, not unusual.

'I'll get the bastards who did this to you,' she whispered.

Priest came back from the bar.

'Are you OK?' he asked.

'Of course not,' sniffed Janja from behind her arm.

'I've brought you a drink,' said Priest, putting a glass of beer down on Janja's table.

'Go away,' said Janja.

'You've seen it, haven't you? Asked Priest.

'What? asked Janja.

'The truth,' said Priest.

'Not sure,' said Janja.

'Will you tell us if you find something?' asked Priest.

Janja took her arm away from her face. Her bloodshot eyes blazed.

'Of course I will,' she screamed.